THE SCARF

Francis Durbridge

WILLIAMS & WHITING

9781912582402

Williams & Whiting (Publishers)
15 Chestnut Grove, Hurstpierpoint,
West Sussex, BN6 9SS

Titles by Francis Durbridge to be published by Williams & Whiting

A Case For Paul Temple
A Game of Murder
A Man Called Harry Brent
A Time of Day
Bat Out of Hell
Breakaway – The Family Affair
Breakaway – The Local Affair
Death Comes to the Hibiscus (stage play – writing as
Nicholas Vane)
La Boutique
Melissa
My Friend Charles
Paul Temple and the Alex Affair
Paul Temple and the Canterbury Case (film script)
Paul Temple and the Conrad Case
Paul Temple and the Curzon Case
Paul Temple and the Geneva Mystery
Paul Temple and the Gilbert Case
Paul Temple and the Gregory Affair
Paul Temple and the Jonathan Mystery
Paul Temple and the Lawrence Affair
Paul Temple and the Madison Mystery
Paul Temple and the Margo Mystery
Paul Temple and the Spencer Affair
Paul Temple and the Sullivan Mystery
Paul Temple and the Vandyke Affair
Paul Temple and Steve
Paul Temple Intervenes
Portrait of Alison
Send for Paul Temple (radio serial)

Send for Paul Temple (stage play)
Step In The Dark
The Broken Horseshoe
The Desperate People
The Doll
The Scarf
The Teckman Biography
The World of Tim Frazer
Three Plays for Radio Volume 1
Three Plays for Radio Volume 2
Tim Frazer and the Salinger Affair
Tim Frazer and the Mellin Forrest Mystery
Twenty Minutes From Rome
Two Paul Temple Plays for Radio
Two Paul Temple Plays for Television

Also by Francis Durbridge and published by Williams & Whiting:

Murder At The Weekend
Murder In The Media

Also published by Williams & Whiting:

Francis Durbridge : The Complete Guide
By Melvyn Barnes

This book reproduces Francis Durbridge's original script together with the list of characters and actors of the BBC programme on the dates mentioned, but the eventual broadcast might have edited Durbridge's script in respect of scenes, dialogue and character names.

FOREWORD

This publication by Williams and Whiting of my father's original script for his television serial *The Scarf* is the first in a series that will bring to fans and the reading public his core work as a playwright and dramatist. Over a career of sixty plus years Francis Durbridge wrote primarily for radio, television and the stage and it was his complicated and ingenious plots and dialogue, within which clues could easily be hidden, where he excelled.

The Scarf was his eighth serial for television, but it has always held a particular place in my affections as I was 10 years of age when it was broadcast, and my parents decided that I was old enough to be allowed to stay up to watch it. Nowadays no doubt I would have been allowed to do so at a younger age but the late 1950s were very different! I remember very well the opening credits with a scarf twisting and turning on its own seemingly in the air. This was achieved by filming in a wind tunnel as this was long before the special effects or computer animation of today. In the background the haunting theme music '*The Girl from Corsica*' by Trevor Duncan played. My father was always involved, with Alan Bromly the producer, in helping choose the theme tunes for his serials and he had a knack of finding music that was beautiful and innocent but by being placed in the context of one of his serials was made to sound gently menacing or mysterious.

I also remember Donald Pleasence playing Detective Inspector Yates brilliantly in a very quiet and unassuming way which of course made him all the more threatening for the villain. He was well thought of as an up-and-coming actor and his performance in *The Scarf* put him on the map. Some years ago, whilst staying at a hotel in France, I saw him sitting at a table having breakfast in the sunshine. I thought of speaking to him but disturbing someone at breakfast I thought not a good idea so did not do so. I regret that now as I would have liked to tell him how good I thought he was in the part which was early on in a highly successful career.

But I am fond of *The Scarf* for another reason. As Melvyn Barnes says in his introduction *The Scarf* was produced all over Europe in six national versions and that was an achievement unique to and typical of my father. Due to his popularity, he was in great demand by the BBC, and this gave him a strong negotiating position which meant that he was able to ensure that the BBC only took English language and Commonwealth broadcast rights for their productions of his work. He could then license productions of the same serial in other countries collecting fees for each one of course. He enjoyed phenomenal European success particularly in Germany where the last episode of *The World of Tim Frazer* still holds the record as the most watched show on German television garnering 93% of the television audience.

The fact that my father understood so well how to license his work had a long-lasting effect on my brother Stephen and I. Our father of course worked from home, so we saw a great deal of him. When sitting round the table for lunch often the discussion would touch upon things related to television or the theatre and thus, we both absorbed a huge amount of knowledge and understanding about the world of media from a young age. It influenced both of us in our later careers with Stephen becoming a film and television agent representing writers and establishing one of the UK's leading agencies in this work called appropriately enough The Agency. As for myself after university I became a solicitor specialising in media work and when in 1977 a client, the author Michael Bond creator of Paddington Bear, asked me to join him to run his merchandising business, I did so and later with my wife Linda established a merchandise licensing agency called Copyrights that represented many of the UK's leading children's characters including Peter Rabbit, The Snowman, Postman Pat, Maisy, Spot, Flower Fairies and of course Paddington Bear which I continue to be involved with to this day.

All of this would probably not have happened had it not been for my father, his knowledge and business acumen. Whilst for many it is his Paul Temple radio serials produced and broadcast from 1938 up to the present day that they remember much of that happened before I was born so for me it is his television serials that I most associate with and that started with *The Scarf*.

I hope that readers will enjoy the original script of *The Scarf* and the other scripts to be published in the series. My thanks to Mike Linane of Williams and Whiting and to Melvyn Barnes for their unstinting enthusiasm and commitment to bringing my father's work to existing and new audiences.

Nicholas Durbridge

INTRODUCTION

Firstly, Francis Durbridge (1912-98) needs to be put into context for those unaware of the considerable breadth of his career. Some present-day enthusiasts might not know that when he turned to television in 1952 he was already the foremost writer of mystery thrillers for BBC radio since the 1930s, and as early as 1938 he had found the niche in which he carved his name after his radio serial *Send for Paul Temple* attracted such public acclaim that he was assured of a series that continued for thirty years and developed an enormous UK and European fanbase.

It is hardly surprising, therefore, that while continuing to write for radio Durbridge joined the rush of writers into the newer medium of television – with the result that in 1952 *The Broken Horseshoe* became the first thriller serial on British television. Indeed this was much later confirmed in an interview with Durbridge (*Radio Times*, 21 October 1971) when he said: "Twenty years ago in the United States, a producer told me that I was wasting my time by not going into television. So that's what I did – I tried to build up a reputation with serials, since I'd vowed never to write a Paul Temple episode for television."

The ground-breaking *The Broken Horseshoe* was reviewed by C.A. Lejeune in her *Observer* column (23 March 1952) in terms that now seem strange. She wrote: "It will be interesting to see how Mr. Durbridge manages his 're-capping' from week to week, for *The Broken Horseshoe* is a true serial and not a series of associated adventures with a beginning, middle and end. The skill with which such a programme can arrange for new viewers to start viewing here, without boring old viewers or wasting time, will achieve much to do with the serial's success. But if it goes on as well as it has begun, I don't intend to miss a Saturday." From this it appears that Durbridge was then regarded as an innovator, although he had been doing that very thing for well over ten years on the radio!

The Scarf was Francis Durbridge's eighth BBC television serial, shown in six thirty-minute episodes from 9 February to 16 March 1959. The producer/director, Alan Bromly, was to remain the guru for most of Durbridge's television serials, just as Martyn C. Webster had been for Durbridge's radio serials. The Durbridge/Bromly television partnership, dating from Durbridge's fourth serial *Portrait of Alison* in 1955, could always be relied upon to provide all the regular ingredients - red herrings galore, cliff-hangers to end each episode, and the certainty that viewers should not believe anything that anyone says.

The Scarf boasted a quality cast – headed by Stephen Murray suffering under suspicion, as he had already done in Durbridge's *My Friend Charles* (1956) and *A Time of Day* (1957). But honorable mention must also be made of Donald Pleasence as Inspector Yates, who contributed his unique "am I nice or nasty?" talents most effectively. Sadly *The Scarf* was never repeated, so it can be assumed that no recording has survived – but it is at least available in another form, because twenty-one years later Durbridge recycled it as *Breakaway - The Local Affair* which is marketed on DVDs in the set *Francis Durbridge Presents Volume 2* (BBC/Madman, 2016).

Francis Durbridge's television trademark involved presenting plots that twisted and turned, while his protagonists struggled in webs spun by masterminds who remained concealed until the final episode. And Durbridge's quintessential Britishness, at a time when many television crime series were imported from the USA, attractively contrasted his sophistication with American sock-in-the-jaw action.

For many years since the 1930s Durbridge's radio serials were broadcast in various European countries, in their own languages and using their own actors. It was therefore obvious that he would also become a great attraction on European television screens, and this began when his sixth television serial (*The Other Man*, 1956) was adopted by German television in 1959. His eighth, *The Scarf*, appeared on German television as *Das Halstuch* (3 – 17 January 1962, six episodes), translated by Marianne de Barde and directed by Hans Quest; on Swedish television as *Halsduken* (20 November - 9 December 1962, eight episodes), translated by Börje Lindell and Ulla Barthels and directed by Hans Lagerkvist; on Finnish television as *Huivi* (4 -15 December 1962, six episodes), translated by Seija Vihma and directed by Juhani Kumpulainen; on Italian television as *La Sciarpa* (11 – 27 March 1963, six episodes), translated by Franca Cancogni and directed by Guglielmo Morandi; on French television as *L'écharpe* (17 – 24 September 1966, two episodes), translated by Abder Isker and Yves Jamiaque and directed by Abder Isker; and on Polish television as *Szal* (12 March – 9 April 1970, three episodes), translated by Kazimierz Piotrowski and directed by Jan Bratkowski.

From this it is clear that *The Scarf* was arguably Durbridge's most popular television serial throughout Europe (maybe vying with *Melissa*), and from *The Other Man* (*Der Andere*, Germany 1959) to *Breakaway* (Addio, Scotland Yard – *Affari locali*, Italy 1985) all Durbridge serials were shown in European countries in their own productions or dubbed UK originals, attracting an unbelievably large body of viewers. And at an early stage he achieved iconic status when German commentators described his serials as *straßenfeger* (street sweepers), because a great swathe of the population stayed at home to listen to them on the radio or watch them on television.

The Scarf was published as a novel (Hodder & Stoughton, October 1960), and in the United States as *The Case of the Twisted Scarf* (Dodd, January 1961). Translations appeared in Germany as *Das Halstuch*; in the Netherlands as *De sjaal*; in Spain as *La bufanda*; in Sweden as *Halsduken*; in Poland as *Szal*; and in Slovakia as *Šatka*. Sadly no English audiobook has yet been produced, which makes this newly discovered original television script particularly worthwhile.

Melvyn Barnes
Author of Francis Durbridge: The Complete Guide (Williams & Whiting, 2018)

THE SCARF

A serial in six episodes

By FRANCIS DURBRIDGE

Broadcast on BBC TV Feb 9th – Mar 16th 1959

CAST:

Rev Nigel Matthews . . . . . . Lockwood West
Edward Collins . . . . Patrick Troughton
Mrs Lloyd . . . . Margery Fleeson
Gerald Quincey . . . . Anthony Valentine
Bill Royd . . . . .Lane Meddick
Alistair Goodman . . . . .Bryan Coleman
Fay Collins . . . . .Norrie Carr
Det. Insp. Yates . . . . Donald Pleasence
Det. Sgt. Jeffreys . . . . Peter Halliday
PC Kent . . . . .Edward Higgins
Marian Hastings . . . . Diana King
Phyllis North . . . . Anne Ridler
Eric . . . . Reginald Barratt
Clifton Morris . . . . Stephen Murray
PC Shaw . . . . .Frank Pemberton
Jill Yates .June Ellis
John Hopedean . . . . Leo Britt
Inspector Rowland . . . . .Fred Ferris
Norman . . . . Neal Arden
Kim Stevens . . . . .Vilma Ann Leslie
Hector .Alan Edmiston
Diana Winston . . . . Jennifer Jayne
Dr. Cousins . . . . .Frank Sieman
Chief Supt Nash . . . . .Arnold Bell
Telegraph boy . . . . Raymond
Show Girl . . . . Diana French
Sgt. Harrison . . . . .Frank Pettitt
P.C. Martin . . . . Stephen Scott

EPISODE ONE

OPEN TO: It is eleven o'clock on a winter's morning. The REVEREND NIGEL MATTHEWS comes out of the front door of Littleshaw Vicarage, walks down the short path to the gate and gets into his waiting car. He is a pleasant, pipe-smoking man in his early forties. He carries a gift parcel, which contains a book. MATTHEWS drives away in the car.

CUT TO: A country lane on the outskirts of Littleshaw. The car appears and draws to a standstill to allow a tractor and trailer to continue its precarious journey out of a nearby field.
The tractor eventually swings on to the road and pulls the trailer past the waiting car. A huge waterproof sheet – a tarpaulin – covers the sugar beet which is on the trailer. The tractor driver – BILL ROYD – grins at MATTHEWS and the VICAR gives a friendly wave of the hand. The car continues down the road.

CUT TO: The Drawing Room of Greensteps, the home of EDWARD COLLINS, near Littleshaw. It is a pleasant room, furnished with period furniture. There is a bay window, a charming fireplace, and in one corner of the room a small grand piano, several unopened letters, birthday cards, and unopened parcels are on the side table which is also used for drinks. EDWARD COLLINS is standing by a drum top table holding the telephone receiver. He is a music teacher; a tense, rather difficult man of about thirty. He is a polio victim and walks with the aid of a stick. The number is ringing out on the telephone but there is obviously no reply.

OPERATOR: (*On the other end*) I'm sorry, sir – there's no reply.

3

EDWARD: Keep ringing …

MRS LLOYD, an elderly housekeeper, enters from the door which leads to a small entrance hall.

MRS LLOYD: Gerald Quincey's here – do you want to see him?

EDWARD: I can't very well give him a lesson if I don't see him! Can I, Mrs Lloyd?

MRS LLOYD: Well, I thought perhaps …

EDWARD: (*A sign of near exasperation*) Ask him in.

MRS LLOYD goes out and a moment later GERALD QUINCEY enters. He is an intelligent, bespectacled youth of about eighteen. He carries a violin case and a small box of chocolates.

GERALD: Hello, Edward! Sorry I'm late …

EDWARD: Are you late?

GERALD: Yes – you said half-past ten. It's nearly eleven o'clock, I'm afraid.

EDWARD: (*Suddenly replacing the receiver*) Well, it doesn't matter, Gerald. I don't feel like work this morning, anyway …

GERALD: (*Disappointed*) Oh …

EDWARD: I didn't sleep very well last night. This blasted leg's been playing me up again. (*Indicating the chocolates*) Is that a birthday present for Fay?

GERALD: Yes.

EDWARD: Well, my charming sister's not here. She didn't come down last night.

GERALD: (*Obviously surprised*) She didn't?

MRS LLOYD enters.

EDWARD: (*Suppressing his annoyance*) No. I don't know what the devil happened. I was expecting her the whole evening, but she

4

never showed up. (*Irritated*) Yes, what is it now, Mrs Lloyd?

MRS LLOYD: Mr Matthews would like to see you.

EDWARD: (*Impatiently*) All right, ask him in.

MRS LLOYD goes out.

EDWARD: (*To Gerald, indicating the chocolates*) Do you want to leave those, or pop round with them again this afternoon?

GERALD: (*Hesitantly*) Well – will Fay be here then?

EDWARD: (*Shrugs*) I don't know, I imagine so. I suppose she'll turn up some time or other.

GERALD: I'll leave them, Edward. (*He puts the box down on the table*) You can say "Many Happy Returns" from me …

REV NIGEL MATTHEWS enters.

MATTHEWS: Good morning, Edward!

EDWARD: Hello, Nigel! You know Gerald Quincey, don't you?

MATTHEWS: Yes, of course. (*Shaking hands*) How are you?

GERALD: I'm very well, thank you, sir. (*To EDWARD*) Well, I'll be off.

EDWARD: Yes. Sorry about the lesson.

GERALD: That's all right, I understand. See you Tuesday.

EDWARD: Yes, of course.

GERALD: I hope you'll feel better by then. (*To MATTHEWS*) Goodbye, Mr Matthews.

MATTHEWS: Goodbye, Gerald.

GERALD goes out into the hall.

MATTHEWS: What's the matter? Has your leg been troubling you again?

EDWARD: A little bit. It's nothing. I should have given him a lesson, I suppose, only …

5

(*Another shrug*) I just don't feel like it this morning.

MATTHEWS: (*Smiling*) And what's annoyed you this morning, Edward?

EDWARD looks at Matthews, then:

EDWARD: It's Fay. She didn't come down last night, after promising me faithfully that she would.

MATTHEWS: Oh dear! I'm sorry. Have you two been quarrelling again?

EDWARD: (*Turning towards MATTHEWS*) No, we haven't. That's just the point. We've been getting on very much better just lately. But I must say, this is pretty inconsiderate, not turning up like this. I had a meal ready and everything.

MATTHEWS: When did you see her last?

EDWARD: About a fortnight ago. But she only telephoned me last weekend and said how much she was looking forward to coming down here. It was her idea, you know. I didn't foster it at all. I said she could do just what the devil she liked for her birthday.

MATTHEWS: That was very magnanimous, Edward.

EDWARD: (*Irritated*) I didn't put it that way. You know what I mean, Nigel!

MATTHEWS: (*Putting his present down on the table*) I gather Fay's not in a play at the moment?

EDWARD: No. And she's not rehearsing, either. (*Crosses to the telephone*) I asked her about that. She seemed a bit despondent, I thought. You know, this business of having a flat in town isn't going to   work out, Nigel. I never thought it would.

MATTHEWS: I thought it was working out rather well.

EDWARD: What do you mean?

MATTHEWS: Well, six months ago you couldn't do a thing for yourself. You were in a wheelchair most of the time. Now you seem to be quite independent. Why, I even saw you shopping the other day, in the High Street.

EDWARD: (*Petulantly, as he lifts the receiver and dials the operator*) I went down to the chemist's. It took me an hour to get there and back. (*On the phone, as the operator answers*) Would you try that number again, please? Mayfair 7351.

MATTHEWS: Is that her flat?

EDWARD nods.

CUT TO: Late afternoon. The tractor and trailer are parked in the main yard at Kingsbury Farm. BILL ROYD crosses from the barn as ALISTAIR GOODMAN, the owner of Kingsbury Farm, comes out of the house. GOODMAN is a well-educated, faintly chuckle-headed man, in his late forties. He wears riding breeches and a well-cut hacking jacket. As he strolls across the yard towards the distant meadow he nods to BILL and points to the trailer.

GOODMAN: I should make a start on that this afternoon, Bill.

BILL gives a friendly nod and starts to unfasten the ropes holding the tarpaulin. He turns back part of the sheet then moves to the rear of the trailer to slacken off the ropes. He returns to the trailer, turns back another section of the tarpaulin and then continues to give the rope his attention. A girl's shoe can be seen protruding from beneath the tarpaulin. Having unfastened the last rope BILL starts on the task of unloading the trailer. He turns back another section of the tarpaulin and then notices the shoe. He stares at the shoe in amazement, and then quickly pulls the tarpaulin off the trailer. The body of FAY COLLINS is revealed. She is an attractive girl of about twenty-five. FAY COLLINS is dead – she has been strangled.

CUT TO: The Farmyard. Twenty minutes later. Two police cars are stationed near the tractor and several plain-clothes men – a doctor, and uniformed police officers are gathered in small groups near the trailer. DETECTIVE INSPECTOR YATES separates himself from the group and slowly strolls across to ALISTAIR GOODMAN and BILL ROYD who are talking to DETECTIVE SERGEANT JEFFREYS who is about thirty; a keen, likeable man. YATES is a determined, unconventional, faintly untidy character.

YATES: You were right, Mr Goodman. Her name's Collins. Fay Collins.
GOODMAN: (*Nervously fingering his tie*) Thought so. Thought I recognised the poor girl. She's a friend of Marian's – my fiancée …
YATES: (*To ROYD*) You say you loaded the trailer up yesterday afternoon?
ROYD: Yes, about four o'clock.
YATES: And you didn't go near the trailer again, or into the field, until eleven o'clock this morning?

ROYD: (*Nodding*) That's right. Then we brought it down here – to the farm.

GOODMAN: We weren't going to unload it until tomorrow, but we got on rather well this afternoon, so I told Bill to make a start on it.

YATES: (*Nodding*) How far is the field from here?

ROYD: (*Pointing*) Well, if you was to go across the meadow it be about four hundred yards. By road – about half a mile.

YATES nods and looks towards the tractor. A small black van has arrived, and two men are carrying a stretcher towards the trailer.

GOODMAN: (*Still fingering his tie, hesitant*) How did she – die, Inspector? What happened, exactly?

YATES turns and looks at GOODMAN.

YATES: She was strangled, Mr Goodman.

CUT TO: The Drawing room of Greensteps.

EDWARD is standing looking out of the window. He is leaning on his stick, his body taut and rigid. YATES is standing near the drum top table, watching him, notebook in hand. After a moment EDWARD turns. He looks tense and unhappy.

EDWARD: (*Curtly*) I'm sorry, Inspector. I shouldn't have lost my temper. I apologise.

YATES: Oh, forget it, sir. I know how I should feel under the circumstances. (*Opening his notebook*) Now, you've told me that you were expecting your sister last night, and that for some unknown reason she didn't turn up …

EDWARD: Yes.

YATES:	(*Consulting the notebook*) You say Miss Collins was an actress and a free-lance model ... you say she had a flat in London ... 28, Welbeck Square ...?
EDWARD:	Yes.
YATES:	(*Looking up from the notebook*) How long has she had this flat, sir?
EDWARD:	About six months.
YATES:	And before that?
EDWARD:	Well, before that she lived here, with me, in Littleshaw.
YATES:	(*Nodding*) Mr Goodman – Mr Alistair Goodman of Kingsbury Farm – identified your sister. He said she was a friend of his fiancée's.
EDWARD:	That's right. That's Marian Hastings. She has a dress shop in the High Street.
YATES:	Was your sister also a friend of Mr Goodman's?
EDWARD:	I don't think so. They'd met, of course, but I wouldn't have called them friends exactly.
YATES:	I see. (*Putting away his notebook*) Mr Collins, tell me – was there anyone here, in Littleshaw, that your sister was particularly friendly with?
EDWARD:	(*Hesitantly*) No.
YATES:	You're sure?
EDWARD:	Yes – I'm quite sure.
YATES:	(*Looks at EDWARD, then nods towards the table*) If your sister had a flat in town, why have several of her friends sent their birthday presents here?
EDWARD:	I think most of these are from local people.

10

YATES:	Then several of the local people knew that she was coming down here?
EDWARD:	Well, yes – obviously.
YATES:	Thank you, Mr Collins. (*He turns towards the door*) Oh, perhaps you'd be kind enough to make a list for me of the people who sent your sister cards and birthday presents?
EDWARD:	Yes. Certainly.
YATES:	There's no hurry. You can drop it in my office tomorrow morning, if you like.
EDWARD:	Very well, Inspector.

YATES nods and goes out. EDWARD stands looking towards the door, then he crosses to the table and starts to mix himself a drink. After a moment he puts down the decanter and buries his head in his hands.

CUT TO: Private Office at Littleshaw Police Station. Morning.

There is a writing desk, armchair, filing cabinet, hat stand, etc. There is a map of the district on the wall by the door. A brown paper parcel in the shape of a box stands on the desk.

YATES comes in, wearing his hat and coat. His manner is brisk and urgent. As he takes off his things a uniformed constable, PC Kent, enters, carrying a manilla folder.

YATES:	(*Indicating the parcel*) What's this?
KENT:	I don't know, sir. It came by the second post. (*He crosses and looks down at the parcel*) It's simply addressed to Littleshaw Police Station.
YATES:	All right. Take it away and open it.
KENT:	Yes, sir.

11

YATES:	(*Unlocking the drawer of his desk*) Has Dr Watts telephoned?
KENT:	No, but he called round about ten minutes ago and left this for you.
YATES:	Oh, thank you. (*Opening the folder*) Tell Jeffreys I want to see him the moment he comes in.
KENT:	Yes, sir.

KENT goes out with the parcel. YATES studies the doctor's report which is in the folder. JEFFREYS enters; he wears outdoor clothes and carries an attaché case.

YATES:	Well?
JEFFREYS:	We've found her handbag. (*He opens the attaché case and takes out a woman's handbag*)
YATES:	(*Rising and coming round from behind the desk*) Where?
JEFFREYS:	In the ditch, about twenty yards from where the tractor was parked. (*He puts the handbag on the desk*)
YATES:	Is Harrison still down there?
JEFFREYS:	Yes; he's taking another look at the footprints.
YATES:	What about those footprints?
JEFFREYS:	There are three sets altogether. Bill Royd's – he's the tractor driver – the girl's, and one other lot we can't account for.
YATES:	Tell Harrison to stop looking and get busy. I want a plaster cast of those straight away.

JEFFREYS smiles and takes a plaster cast of the footprints out of his attaché case. YATES takes the cast and gives JEFFREYS a look.

YATES:	Good.

YATES examines the cast.

YATES: Did Harrison make any comment?

JEFFREYS: (*Pointing*) Only about the size. He's marked them.

YATES: Yes. (*He puts the cast on the desk*) Well – how did you get on, Jeff?

JEFFREYS: (*Sitting on the arm of the armchair: shaking his head*) I must have questioned a hundred people since last night. No one saw Fay Collins on Wednesday night – or, if they did, they're keeping quiet about it.

YATES: What about that friend of hers, the one with the dress shop?

JEFFREYS: Miss Hastings – Goodman's fiancée?

YATES: Yes.

JEFFREYS: (*Shaking his head*) She's away at the moment, on holiday somewhere.

YATES: (*Indicating the folder on the desk*) Well, I've had the doctor's report. He says it happened some time after nine and not later than ten-thirty.

JEFFREYS: Ten-thirty?

YATES: Yes. He seems to think that whoever did it used a scarf, or a sash of some kind. I'm inclined to agree with him because …

JEFFREYS: (*Interrupting him*) A scarf?

YATES: Yes.

JEFFREYS: (*Quietly, surprised*) That's very odd.

YATES: What do you mean?

JEFFREYS picks up the handbag and tips the contents on to the desk. There is a lipstick, handkerchief, mirror, comb, several coins and a telegram. He picks up the telegram and opens it.

13

JEFFREYS: (*Reading*) "Many thanks for the scarf. Love. Terry."

YATES stares at him for a moment, then takes the telegram out of his hand. There is a pause.

YATES: (*Still looking at the telegram, puzzled*) Fay Collins. 28. Wellbeck Square, SW1 … January, 4th …

JEFFREYS: That's five days ago.

YATES: Yes. Sent from Oxford Street Post Office. (*Thoughtfully*) I'll check this, Jeff …

YATES moves round the desk, still looking at the telegram. After a moment he puts it down.

JEFFREYS: That's very curious, isn't it – in view of the doctor's report?

YATES: (*Quietly, still looking at the telegram*) Yes … Yes, it certainly is …

The door opens and PC Kent enters.

KENT: Excuse me, sir. Mr Collins would like to see you.

YATES: Wait a moment and then show him in.

KENT: Yes, sir.

PC KENT goes out.

YATES: (*Seriously*) Jeff, do you know a man called John Hopedean?

JEFFREYS: (*Nodding*) Yes. Lives in Bellmore Avenue.

YATES: That's right. What do you know about him?

JEFFREYS: He's a commercial artist. Freelance. Pretty well off, I believe. Married. No children. Why do you ask?

YATES: I was talking to my wife about this affair. She said Hopedean used to be very friendly with Fay Collins. Apparently, it was fairly common gossip at one time.

14

JEFFREYS: Yes, I believe it was. Whether there was any truth in it or not I don't know. Anyway, I checked on Hopedean this morning. He was out, but I saw his wife.

YATES: Well?

JEFFREYS: She said they were both in on Wednesday night – all night. He was working, she was watching the television.

YATES nods. The door opens and PC KENT and EDWARD enter.

YATES: Come in, Mr Collins. This is Sergeant Jeffreys.

JEFFREYS: (*Rising*) Good morning, sir.

EDWARD: Good morning. (*To YATES*) I've got that list you wanted. (*He takes a piece of notepaper out of his wallet and hands it to YATES*)

YATES: Thank you, Mr Collins. (*He glances at the notepaper*) That's very kind of you. (*Going back behind his desk and indicating the armchair*) Do sit down, sir.

EDWARD sits in the armchair and as he does so, he notices the handbag on the desk.

EDWARD: You've found my sister's handbag, then?

YATES: Yes. Sergeant Jeffreys found it.

EDWARD: Where?

JEFFREYS: (*Quietly*) It was in the field, sir.

YATES: (*Picking up the telegram and offering it to EDWARD*) This telegram was in the handbag. It's obviously from a friend of your sister's. Someone called Terry.

EDWARD: (*Obviously recognising the name*) Terry? (*He takes the telegram*)

15

YATES looks across at JEFFREYS for a moment.

YATES: Have you any idea who sent that? Who
            Terry is?

EDWARD: (*Looking up from the telegram*) No, I'm
            afraid I haven't. But – (*Putting the
            telegram on the desk*) Whoever he is, he's
            obviously very well off …

YATES: Why? What makes you say that, sir?

*EDWARD takes a flat jewellery case out of his overcoat
pocket.*

EDWARD: He sent my sister a birthday present.
            (*Shaking his head*) It's quite incredible
            … The sort of present a girl dreams about.
            (*He opens the case and takes out a
            diamond bracelet*)

JEFFREYS gives a low whistle of admiration.

YATES: (*Picking up the bracelet*) That certainly is
            a birthday present.

JEFFREYS: Was there a letter with it, sir – or a card?

EDWARD: (*Taking a card from his pocket*) Yes, there
            was this. But there's no address or
            anything on it. It just says – (*Looking at
            the card*) – "From Terry – with love, and
            because of La Lavencher."

*EDWARD hands the card to YATES who looks at it and
then hands it across to JEFFREYS.*

YATES: (*Examining the bracelet again*) I suppose
            they are diamonds?

EDWARD: Yes, I took it to Milton's in the High
            Street. They're diamonds. It's worth the
            best part of a thousand pounds.

JEFFREYS: (*Looking at the card*) La Lavencher …
            Where is that?

EDWARD: It's a village in France – in Haute Savoir.

16

YATES: Have you been there?

EDWARD: No, I'd never even heard of it, but just as I
            was leaving the house, Mr Matthews
            called. I showed him the note and we
            looked the place up in a Gazetteer.

JEFFREYS: Had your sister ever been there?

EDWARD: No, I don't think she'd been further south
            than Paris.

YATES: Did you show Mr Matthews the bracelet?

EDWARD: Yes, it was his idea that I took it to
            Milton's. (*With the suggestion of a smile*)
            We weren't sure whether it was genuine or
            not.

YATES: I see. Well, I'd like to keep it; for the time
            being at any rate.

EDWARD: Yes, of course. (*He rises*)

YATES also rises and moves round to the front of the desk.

YATES: (*Quite pleasantly*) Mr Collins, I was in
            London this morning and I took the
            opportunity of visiting your sister's flat.

EDWARD: Indeed?

YATES: Yes. I was very impressed, sir. Still, I
            imagine you've been there?

EDWARD: (*Irritated*) You imagine wrong, Inspector.
            I didn't approve of Fay taking the flat in
            the first place, so I saw no reason why I
            should go there.

YATES: Oh. Oh, I see. Well, it's certainly a very
            nice one. Miss Collins was paying thirty-
            five guineas a week for it.

EDWARD: Was she?

YATES: Yes. Could she afford thirty-five guineas a
            week?

17

EDWARD: Well, if she was paying it, I imagine she
            could, Inspector.
YATES: (*Smiling*) That doesn't always follow.
EDWARD: (*Holding out his hand: terminating the
            interview*) If anything develops, or you
            want to get in touch with me, you know
            where I am.
YATES: (*Shaking hands*) Yes, of course, and thank
            you for coming along, Mr Collins. I'll see
            you out, sir.
JEFFREYS: Good morning, sir.
EDWARD: Good morning.

*EDWARD goes out followed by YATES. JEFFREYS looks
towards the door and thoughtfully rubs the back of his
head, a gesture implying that EDWARD COLLINS is not
the easiest of people to get on with. He then crosses to the
desk and picks up the bracelet. He is looking at the
bracelet when KENT enters.*

KENT: Excuse me, Sergeant, there's a young chap
            here called Gerald Quincey. He wants to
            see the Inspector.
JEFFREYS: All right, show him in.

*KENT goes to the door and beckons GERALD who is
waiting outside. As GERALD enters, KENT goes out.
JEFFREYS puts down the bracelet.*

JEFFREYS: Hello, Gerald! How are you?
GERALD: (*Nervously*) I'm all right, thank you,
            Sergeant. I wanted to see Inspector Yates.
JEFFREYS: Yes – well, he'll be back in a minute.
            Anything I can do?
GERALD: It's terrible about Fay Collins, isn't it?
JEFFREYS: It certainly is.
GERALD: That's – that's what I want to see the
            Inspector about.

18

JEFFREYS:	About the murder?
GERALD:	Yes, I don't know whether it's important or not, but – (*Hesitating, then:*) – I saw her on Wednesday night.

YATES appears in the doorway.

JEFFREYS:	(*Astonished*) You – what?
GERALD:	I – I saw her …

YATES comes into the room closing the door behind him. He has overheard GERALD's remark.

YATES:	What is this? What's this all about?
JEFFREYS:	This is Gerald Quincey. He says he saw Fay Collins on Wednesday night.
YATES:	(*Quickly, turning to GERALD*) Where?
GERALD:	Near Layton Avenue …
YATES:	What time was this?
GERALD:	About half past eight.
YATES:	Are you sure it was Miss Collins?
GERALD:	Yes, I'm positive …
YATES:	Did you know her – was she a friend of yours?
GERALD:	Yes. I've known her for years. Edward – her brother – gives me music lessons.

JEFFREYS looks at YATES and nods. YATES sites on the corner of the desk, looking at GERALD.

YATES:	All right, Gerald. Now tell me exactly what happened …
GERALD:	Well, there's not much to tell. I'd been to the local tennis club – there was a ping-pong tournament – and I was driving home. Just as I turned into Oxford Close, I saw Fay. She was on the other side of the road, on the corner, near Layton Avenue.
YATES:	Was she alone?
GERALD:	Yes.

19

YATES: You're sure?

GERALD: Yes, I'm positive.

YATES: Did she see you?

GERALD: No, I don't think so. (*Shaking his head*) No, I'm sure she didn't.

JEFFREYS: Well, what was she doing exactly?

GERALD: She was just stood on the corner of the road.

YATES: Waiting for someone?

GERALD: Yes – I suppose so. I don't know, I didn't really think about it.

YATES: (*Quietly*) Have you told anyone else about this?

GERALD: No. I nearly told Edward – Mr Collins – but I thought perhaps …

JEFFREYS: When did you see Mr Collins?

GERALD: Yesterday morning. I was supposed to have a music lesson, but he was in a pretty foul temper because Fay hadn't shown up. It was her birthday, you know.

YATES: Yes. (*Quietly*) Why didn't you tell Mr Collins that you'd see his sister the night before?

GERALD: Well, I didn't really think it was any of my business. You see, Edward and Fay haven't always got on well together, and I thought perhaps she may possibly have stayed the night with someone else.

YATES: Someone else?

GERALD: Well, some friend or other …

YATES: (*Quietly, watching him*) I see.

GERALD: Besides … (*He hesitates*)

YATES: (*Pleasantly*) Go on …

GERALD: Well, Edward's a funny chap. (*Quickly*) Don't misunderstand me, I like him – I like him enormously – I mean he's an awfully good teacher and all that. But if you happen to say the wrong thing or get on the wrong side of him …

YATES: (*Smiling*) I know exactly what you mean, Gerald.

There is a knock on the door and PC KENT enters. He carries a man's shoe in his hand and looks faintly amused.

YATES: What is it, Kent?

KENT: I'm very sorry, sir, but I've just opened that parcel and I thought …

YATES: Well?

KENT: (*Puzzled*) Well, I don't know whether it's a joke, Inspector, but – this was inside.

YATES and JEFFREYS move to KENT. YATES takes the shoe and looks at it. It is a fairly large, reasonably new, man's shoe, covered in dust and mud. YATES looks at JEFFREYS, then across at KENT.

YATES: Was there anything else in the parcel?

KENT: No, sir, nothing.

YATES: Where was it posted?

KENT: I – I don't know, sir.

YATES: Bring me the paper, the wrapper, the string, the whole lot …

KENT: Yes, sir.

KENT goes out. YATES looks at the shoe, then turns and picks up the plaster cast from the desk. He holds them close together, studying their respective sizes, then slowly he places the cast on the shoe: it fits perfectly. YATES looks up and across at JEFFREYS.

CUT TO: Late Afternoon. A Sunbeam Rapier draws to a standstill outside of Littleshaw Police Station. MARIAN HASTINGS gets out of the car. She is a smartly dressed,

21

sophisticated woman of about thirty. MARIAN walks very quickly towards the main entrance of the Police Station.

CUT TO: YATES' Office. Day.
YATES is sitting at his desk, writing a report. PC KENT enters.

YATES: (*Looking up*) Yes – what is it?
KENT: A Miss Hastings wants to see you, sir.
YATES: (*Putting down his pen*) Miss Hastings? Isn't that the woman with the dress shop?
KENT: Yes, sir.
YATES: I thought she was abroad?
KENT: Well, she's outside at the moment, sir.
YATES gets up and walks round to the front of his desk.
YATES: All right. Show her in.
KENT goes out. YATES leans against his desk looking towards the door. KENT returns.
KENT: (*In the doorway*) Miss Hastings.
MARIAN HASTINGS comes into the room. KENT closes the door on his way out.
YATES: (*Holding out his hand*) Miss Hastings, I don't think we've met before. I'm Detective Inspector Yates.
MARIAN: (*A shade tense; nervously shaking hands*) Good afternoon.
YATES: (*Indicating a chair*) Please – do sit down.
MARIAN: (*Sitting*) I don't know whether you know it or not, but I've been away. I only got back this morning.
YATES: (*Taking his position at the desk*) Yes, so I understand. Your fiancé, Mr Goodman, told me that you were abroad.
MARIAN: Yes, I know. Inspector, I only heard yesterday about the murder – about Fay. I

22

	bought an English newspaper in Chamonix … I – I was absolutely staggered.
YATES:	Yes, I imagine you were.
MARIAN:	The paper said she was murdered on January 7th …
YATES:	That's right. Wednesday of last week. Six days ago.
MARIAN:	(*Hesitantly*) Well – I saw Fay. I saw Fay Collins the night she was murdered.
YATES:	(*Surprised*) Where?
MARIAN:	Here – in Littleshaw.
YATES:	Go on, Miss Hastings.
MARIAN:	Well, it was about a quarter to nine. I was driving to town. You see, I stayed the night in London with a friend of mine, and then flew to Geneva the next morning.
YATES:	I understand. Go on …
MARIAN:	Well, I saw Fay and waved to her. She was standing on the corner of Layton Avenue.
YATES:	Did she see you?
MARIAN:	Yes, of course she did. She waved back.
YATES:	Was she alone?
MARIAN:	(*Shaking her head*) No, there was a man with her.
YATES:	Did you recognise him?
MARIAN:	No. I'd never seen him before.
YATES:	You're sure of that?
MARIAN:	Yes, I'm quite sure.
YATES:	Would you recognise him again if you saw him?
MARIAN:	Yes – at least, I think so. I knew you'd ask that question, of course. I've been thinking about it all the way here. (*A moment, a*

23

	shade tense, but confident) Yes, I think I would. I think I would, Inspector.
YATES:	Good … Now try and give me a description of him.
MARIAN:	Oh dear …
YATES:	(*Trying to control his impatience*) Now don't worry, Miss Hastings. Take it easy – there's no hurry. (*He rises and comes round to the front of the desk*) How tall was he?
MARIAN:	About six foot …
YATES:	Clean shaven?
MARIAN:	Yes …
YATES:	What sort of age?
MARIAN:	Oh … Thirty-eight – or nine – early forties perhaps …
YATES:	(*Nodding*) Good. Now what was he wearing, can you remember?
MARIAN:	(*Thoughtfully*) Yes. He had a dark overcoat, a black Homburg hat … And I think he was wearing gloves, but I'm not sure … (*Suddenly*) Oh, and he had a scarf … Yes, I remember that now … (*Nodding*) He was wearing a scarf.

YATES looks at MARIAN HASTINGS.

CUT TO: MARIAN'S Dress Shop. Day

It is a tiny salon, with a window at right angles to the main entrance to the shop. An alcove leads to a small office, there is a large, ornate, French style table in the centre of the room. There are several chairs, fitted cupboards and drawers. An etching – by John Hopedean – is on the wall near the alcove.

PHYLLIS NORTH, a young assistant, is arranging an evening gown on a display stand, ready for the window. After a little while MARIAN comes out of the office carrying a bunch of flowers and a vase. She puts them down on the table.

MARIAN: Get me a newspaper, Phyllis. There's some in the cupboard over there.

PHYLLIS crosses, opens the cupboard, and takes out several newspapers. She spreads them out on the table for MARIAN and then returns to the dress. MARIAN opens the bunch of flowers, preparing them for the vase.

PHYLLIS: What about the hat, Miss Hastings? Are we going to leave it in the window?

MARIAN: Yes, I think so.

PHYLLIS: Don't you think it'll clash?

MARIAN: (*Smiling*) Well, if it does, we'll take it out, Phyllis.

PHYLLIS: (*Touching the dress*) This is lovely, isn't it? Such a nice colour. He does make some wonderful things. (*Walking round the stand*) Do you know who would have liked this? … Fay Collins … She'd have looked lovely in it.

MARIAN: (*Quietly; still arranging the flowers*) She looked lovely in almost anything.

PHYLLIS: Yes, that's true. (*Thoughtfully*) You know, I don't reckon they'll ever catch him – the chap who did it, I mean. It's over a fortnight now, isn't it? (*A moment*) My Dad says the police are hopeless – he says they couldn't even catch a cold.

PHYLLIS looks at the dress again and stands admiring it – imagining herself wearing it. MARIAN smiles and continues to fill the vase with flowers, glancing down at the newspaper on the table as she does so. After a moment, something in the newspaper attracts her attention. She puts down the flowers she is holding and stares at it. Suddenly, she pushes the remaining flowers to one side and picks up the newspaper. PHYLLIS stops admiring herself and with a puzzled look, moves to the table.

PHYLLIS: What is it?

We see the newspaper which is in Marian's hand. She is looking at a photograph of passengers leaving a B.O.A.C. comet at London Airport. A distinguished, serious-looking man in his early forties is in the centre of the group. He is wearing a scarf. The newspaper caption reads: "New York – London. Record Breaking Passengers".

CUT TO: YATES' Office. Day.

YATES is sitting at his desk facing MARIAN who is stood, looking down at him. In his hand is the newspaper and he is looking at the photograph.

YATES: (*Unable to conceal his excitement*) Are you sure?

A moment, then MARIAN gives a little nod.

YATES: You're sure that this is the man you saw with Fay Collins?

MARIAN: (*Tensely*) I'm positive.

YATES: Thank you, Miss Hastings!

YATES folds the newspaper and rises from the desk.

MARIAN: (*Nervously*) Who is he? Do you know?

YATES: (*Grimly*) No – but we'll very soon find out!

(*He crosses and collects his hat and coat from the stand*)

CUT TO: The Front Door in the carpeted corridor of a West End block of flats.

A small wall table, bearing a bowl of flowers, stands near the door. There is a bell push and a framed card. The card reads: "Mr Clifton Morris." A gloved hand appears and presses the bell push. After a moment the door is opened by ERIC. He is about thirty, wears a white house-jacket, and dark trousers.

YATES: (*Facing the door*) Good evening …
ERIC: Good evening, sir.
YATES: Is Mr Morris in?
ERIC: Yes, but I'm afraid he can't see anyone at the moment.
YATES: (*Interrupting him*) Tell Mr Morris I'd very much like to have a word with him. I'm Detective Inspector Yates.
ERIC: Oh, I'm sorry, sir! Yes, of course! Come in, Inspector!

YATES looks at ERIC, a shade surprised, then enters the flat.

CUT TO: The Drawing Room of CLIFTON MORRIS' Flat. Evening.
This is a pleasantly, beautifully furnished, bachelor apartment.

YATES enters, followed by ERIC, and as he does so, CLIFTON MORRIS comes out of the bedroom. He is the man in the newspaper photograph. He is in evening dress and is actually putting on his dinner jacket as he comes into the room. He is still in his slippers. His manner indicates that he is late for an appointment.

MORRIS: Eric, where on earth have you put my shoes? I've been looking all over for … (*He stops, stares at YATES*)
ERIC: This is a Police Inspector, sir.
MORRIS: (*Apparently not surprised*) Oh, good evening.

27

YATES: Good evening, sir.

MORRIS: Well – is there any news? Have you found it?

YATES: (*Puzzled*) Found what, sir?

MORRIS: Why, the briefcase!

YATES: Have you lost your briefcase, sir?

MORRIS: Why, of course, I've lost it, and my overcoat! They were stolen – taken from my car earlier this evening. (H*e looks back at ERIC, then back at YATES*) I reported it to the local police a couple of hours ago.

ERIC: (*To YATES*) I thought that's what you'd called about.

YATES: No, I'm sorry, I'm afraid I know nothing about this. My name is Yates – Detective Inspector Yates. I'm from Littleshaw.

MORRIS: Littleshaw – in Hertfordshire?

YATES: Yes, sir. Do you know it?

MORRIS: Yes, I do. I've got a house in Birkendale – that's about ten miles away.

YATES: (*Nodding*) That's right.

MORRIS: (*Quietly*) Eric, find my shoes …

ERIC: (*Looking at YATES*) Yes, sir.

ERIC goes into the bedroom.

MORRIS: (*Curious*) What can I do for you, Inspector?

YATES: I'm investigating a murder case. You may have read about it. About a fortnight ago a girl called Fay Collins was found murdered – strangled.

MORRIS: Yes, of course. I've read quite a lot about it.

YATES: (*Pleasantly*) Did you know Miss Collins, sir?

MORRIS: (*Surprised*) Me?

YATES: Yes, sir.

MORRIS: Why, no.

YATES: You'd never met?

28

MORRIS: I don't think so. I certainly don't remember meeting her.

YATES: I think you'd have remembered her – if you had met. She was an extremely pretty girl.

MORRIS: During the course of my work, I meet a great many pretty girls, Inspector.

YATES: I wish I could say the same, sir.

MORRIS: (*Smiling*) Don't misunderstand me. I'm not a film producer or anything like that. But I own two fashion magazines, so naturally …

YATES: (*Interrupting him*) Yes, I know, sir. I looked you up in "Who's Who" before I came here.

MORRIS: (*A shade surprised*) Oh … Oh, you did?

YATES: (*Looking round the apartment*) Yes. I was very impressed by your activities, Mr Morris. You must be a very busy man.

MORRIS: So busy, I'd like you to get to the point, Inspector. What's this all about?

YATES looks at MORRIS, then takes a folded newspaper from his overcoat pocket.

YATES: (*Holding out the newspaper*) Have you seen this before?

MORRIS: (*Looking at the newspaper*) Why, yes. It was taken last week when I arrived back from New York.

YATES: That's right, sir. (*A moment*) How long were you in the States?

MORRIS: A fortnight.

YATES: Exactly a fortnight?

MORRIS: I left London on January the 8th.

YATES: (*Looking at him*) Miss Collins was murdered on the night of January the 7th.

MORRIS: Was she?

YATES: Yes.

29

MORRIS: I'll take your word for it.

YATES: Where were you that night, sir – the night before you left for New York?

MORRIS: I was here, in London. Why?

YATES: Can you remember what you did that evening?

MORRIS: Yes, of course I can. (*Thoughtfully*) I left the office at about half past six, had dinner at the Club, and went to a cinema.

YATES: Which cinema?

MORRIS: The one in Curzon Street.

YATES: Were you alone?

MORRIS: Why, yes.

YATES: Did anyone see you at the cinema?

MORRIS: (*Astonished, interrupting him*) Look, what is this? (*He indicates the newspaper*) What's this all about?

YATES: A woman called Marian Hastings says she saw you in Littleshaw, talking to Fay Collins, on the night of January 7th – the night of the murder. She identified you from this photograph.

MORRIS: But that's absurd! I wasn't anywhere near Littleshaw.

YATES: Miss Hastings seems pretty positive, sir.

MORRIS: She may be positive – she's also mistaken. (*Shaking his head*) It certainly wasn't me she saw.

YATES: I see. (*He puts the newspaper back in his pocket*)

MORRIS: Who is this Miss Hastings, anyway?

YATES: She's quite well known in Littleshaw. She keeps a dress shop in the High Street. She's engaged to a farmer called Goodman.

MORRIS: Goodman?

YATES: Yes. Alistair Goodman. Kingsbury Farm. You
          may have heard of him?

MORRIS: No; the only person I know in Littleshaw is the
         vicar – Matthews. We were at Cambridge
         together.

YATES: Yes, I know Mr Matthews, of course. How long
          is it since you were in that part of the world,
          sir?

MORRIS: Oh, about four months, I should say – perhaps
         even longer.

YATES: I thought you said you had a house in
          Birkendale?

MORRIS: I have, but I don't go there very often. I also
         have a house at Angmering; I go there even
         less.

YATES: (*Pleasantly*) Well, thank you, Mr Morris. I'm
          sorry to have troubled you. (*He turns, then
          apparently remembers something*) Oh, there's
          just one point.

MORRIS: Yes?

YATES: (*Tapping the newspaper in his pocket*) You're
          wearing a scarf in this photograph. That's
          partly why Miss Hastings thought she
          recognised you. The man she saw was wearing
          a scarf – one like yours.

MORRIS: Oh, I see.

YATES: Do you think I could have a look at it, sir?

MORRIS: (*Smiling*) My scarf?

YATES: Yes.

MORRIS: (*Pleasantly*) Why, of course. I'll get it for you.
         (*He moves towards the bedroom then suddenly
         stops*) Oh, I'm sorry, Inspector. I've just
         remembered. I was wearing it this afternoon.
         It's in my overcoat pocket.

ERIC comes out of the bedroom, carrying a pair of patent leather shoes, an overcoat and a Homburg hat. The telephone starts to ring.

YATES: (*A moment, then lightly*) Oh, well, that's all right. Never mind, sir. It's not important.

ERIC puts the shoes, and hat, and coat on the settee, then crosses to the telephone.

ERIC: (*On the phone*) Regent 9476.

SERGEANT: (*On the other end of the line*) This is Savile Row Police Station. Can I speak to Mr Morris?

ERIC: One moment, please. (*To MORRIS*) It's the Police, sir.

MORRIS: Oh. (*To YATES*) Excuse me.

MORRIS crosses and takes the receiver. ERIC looks at YATES with curiosity and returns to the bedroom. During the following conversation YATES crosses, casually picks up one of the shoes and glances inside it.

MORRIS: (*On the phone*) Clifton Morris speaking.

SERGEANT: Oh, good evening, sir. Savile Row Police Station here. We've got your briefcase, Mr Morris.

MORRIS: (*Pleased*) Oh, splendid!

SERGEANT: But I'm afraid we haven't had any luck with the overcoat, sir.

MORRIS: What about the cigarette lighter?

SERGEANT: No, I'm sorry. That was in the coat, wasn't it, sir?

MORRIS: Yes, I think so.

SERGEANT: Well, we've got a description of it. We'll let you know the moment we hear anything.

MORRIS: Thank you. I'll pick the brief case up in about fifteen minutes.

SERGEANT: Very good, Mr Morris.

MORRIS: Oh – where did you find the case?

SERGEANT: A schoolboy found it, sir, in Regent's Park – about twenty minutes ago.

MORRIS: Well – thank you very much.

SERGEANT: Goodnight, sir.

MORRIS: Goodnight.

MORRIS replaces the receiver. He then crosses over to YATES.

YATES: They've found the case?

MORRIS: Yes.

YATES: What about the coat?

MORRIS: (*Shaking his head and crossing to the settee*) No …

YATES: How did you come to lose these things, sir?

MORRIS: I'd been to a meeting; I was in a devil of a hurry, so I threw the things into the back of the car. I called in at my office in Park Lane and when I came out, they'd gone. (*He looks at his wristlet watch*) I don't give a damn about the coat, but I've lost my cigarette lighter. (*He picks up one of the shoes*) Now, if you'll excuse me, I've got an appointment at eight o'clock, and I'm late already. (*He puts the shoe on*)

YATES: Yes, of course.

ERIC comes out of the bedroom.

MORRIS: Goodnight.

YATES: Goodnight, Mr Morris. And thank you very much.

33

MORRIS: (*Looking up*) I'm sorry I wasn't more helpful.

YATES: On the contrary, you've been most helpful.

YATES crosses to the door with ERIC.

MORRIS: (*Quietly*) Oh, Inspector …

YATES turns.

YATES: Yes?

MORRIS: (*Holding up the other shoe*) These are a little on the tight side. I take nine-and-a-half.

YATES: (*After a moment, blandly*) Thank you, Mr Morris.

YATES goes out with ERIC. MORRIS looks towards the hall then slowly, thoughtfully, puts on the shoe. ERIC returns.

ERIC: (*Quietly*) I'm very sorry, sir. I thought he'd called about the briefcase.

MORRIS: That's all right, Eric.

MORRIS rises; picks up his overcoat. ERIC crosses and helps him on with it.

MORRIS: I shall be back about eleven. If there's anything really important, you can get me at the restaurant.

ERIC: Yes, sir. That's the one in Dover Street?

MORRIS: That's right. (*He indicates the table*) It's in the book. Le Lavencher. Goodnight.

ERIC: Goodnight, sir.

MORRIS crosses towards the hall.

CUT TO: The Drawing Room of Greensteps. The Following Morning.

EDWARD is at the piano, playing a Beethoven Sonata, there is an empty coffee cup on the piano, and an ash tray with several cigarette ends. He is wearing a dressing gown over pyjamas and looks distinctly annoyed. After a moment the telephone rings. He continues playing but the ringing persists. EDWARD rises and crosses to the phone. As he picks up the receiver, a self-conscious GERALD QUINCEY enters the room. He carries his violin case and is quite obviously late for his lesson again. EDWARD gives him a look and turns his back on him.

EDWARD: (*On the phone*) Hello? … Littleshaw 134.

YATES: (*On the other end of the line*) Mr Collins?

EDWARD: Speaking.

YATES: This is Yates.

EDWARD: Oh, good morning, Inspector.

YATES: Good morning. I'm sorry if I've disturbed you.

EDWARD: What is it? What can I do for you?

YATES: I was in London last night, sir, and I met an old friend of your sister's – a Mr Clifton Morris.

EDWARD: Clifton Morris?

YATES: Yes. (*Politely*) He was a friend of your sister's wasn't he, Mr Collins?

EDWARD: I don't know. I've certainly never heard of him.

YATES: (*Pleasantly; yet surprised*) Haven't you, sir?

EDWARD: No.

YATES: (*Still pleasant, but with emphasis*) Are you sure?

EDWARD: Yes, I'm quite sure.

YATES: Oh, well, in that case I'm very sorry to have bothered you. Goodbye, sir.

YATES replaces his receiver. EDWARD looks puzzled by the abrupt termination of the conversation. He slowly

35

replaces his receiver, then suddenly becomes aware of the fact that GERALD is stood watching him.

GERALD: (*Nervously*) I'm awfully sorry, Edward. I do apologise.

EDWARD: (*With sarcasm*) For what, Gerald, do you apologise?

GERALD: Why, for being late …

EDWARD: But you're improving! You were twenty minutes late on Tuesday – you're only a quarter of an hour this morning.

GERALD: Yes, I know, but … I suddenly remembered I had to change my mother's library book, and when I got back to the house …

EDWARD: (*Interrupting him*) Tell me – why is that unique shuttle-cock arrangement between your mother, yourself and the public library confined to Tuesdays and Fridays?

GERALD: I don't know, Edward.

EDWARD: I think I should find out if I were you.

GERALD: I'm really awfully sorry …

EDWARD: Now what would you like to do this morning – the Paganini?

GERALD: (*Pleased*) Yes, I would.

EDWARD: Then I suggest we make a start.

GERALD crosses and puts his violin case on the piano.

GERALD: Was that the Inspector?

EDWARD: Yes.

GERALD: (*Curious*) Did he mention a man called Clifton Morris?

EDWARD: (*At the piano*) Yes, he did. Why?

GERALD: (*Puzzled; shaking his head*) I've heard that name before.

EDWARD: Have you, Gerald?

GERALD: Yes. Isn't he a publisher or something?

EDWARD: I don't know.

GERALD: Yes, I think he is. (*Thoughtfully*) Clifton Morris …

EDWARD: (*Quietly; watching GERALD*) You've probably seen his name or read about him somewhere.

GERALD: (*His thoughts elsewhere*) Yes, I suppose that's it. I suppose I must have done.

EDWARD: (*Impatiently*) Come along, Gerald! Let's get started – we're late already.

GERALD: Yes, of course. Sorry, Edward.

GERALD opens the case and takes out his violin. Suddenly he hesitates, then staring at the case in obvious surprise, he puts the instrument down on the piano. Puzzled and bewildered he slowly extracts another object from the violin case. He looks at it in astonishment. EDWARD turns, about to speak to GERALD, then stops, staring at him in surprise.

EDWARD: (*After a moment*) Is that yours?

GERALD: (*Shaking his head; bewildered*) No … No, Edward …

GERALD looks down at what he is holding. It is a scarf.

END OF EPISODE ONE

EPISODE TWO

OPEN TO: The Drawing Room at Greensteps. Day.

*YATES is standing by the piano examining the scarf.
EDWARD COLLINS and GERALD QUINCEY are
watching him.*

EDWARD: … It's probably not important, Inspector,
              but I remembered that telegram about the
              scarf and the doctor's report saying she'd
              been strangled with one.

GERALD: (*Surprised*) Fay – strangled with a scarf?
              (*He looks at YATES*) Is this true, sir?

YATES: (*Quietly*) Yes. Either a scarf or a sash of
              some kind. (*He moves towards GERALD*)
              Now you say you've never seen this
              before and it wasn't in the violin case
              when you left the house?

GERALD: Yes, sir.

YATES: What did you do when you left home? Did
              you come straight here?

GERALD: Well, I started out to come here, and then I
              remembered I hadn't changed my
              mother's library book, so I went to the
              library.

YATES: And then what?

GERALD: I drove back home, dropped in the book,
              and came here.

YATES: How long were you in the library?

GERALD: About five minutes.

YATES: And where was the violin case?

GERALD: In my car. I left the car in the car park.

YATES: Did you see anyone you know?

GERALD: I saw Mr Goodman.

YATES: Mr Alistair Goodman – Kingsbury Farm?

GERALD: Yes.

41

YATES:	Where did you see him?
GERALD:	He was just driving out of the car park.
YATES:	Did he speak to you?
GERALD:	Oh, yes – he always does. Says the same thing every time. "Still on the fiddle, Gerald?"
YATES:	Did you see anyone else?
GERALD:	No. (*An afterthought*) Oh, the vicar, of course – Mr Matthews.
YATES:	When did you see Mr Matthews?
GERALD:	When I got back home. He was just leaving. He'd dropped in to have a chat with my mother.
YATES:	And when you got back home – with the library book – I presume you left the violin case in the car and simply dashed into the house?
GERALD:	Yes, that's right. I was only in the house two minutes.
YATES:	Well, thank you, Gerald. (*To EDWARD*) And thank you for telephoning, sir. (*He crosses to the door*)
EDWARD:	(*Indicating the scarf*) What will you do with that, Inspector – send it to Scotland Yard?
YATES:	Eventually, sir. (*He nods to GERALD and goes out*)

CUT TO: The Living room of YATES' Cottage, Littleshaw. Afternoon.

This is a comfortable lived-in room, with an ingle-nook fireplace, period furniture, and a raised alcove on the extreme right. This alcove is almost separate from the rest of the room and is used as a dining room. The main entrance to the cottage is through a hall off to the right, and there is a door to the left leading to a modern kitchen. There is also a second door leading to a bedroom. The kitchen door is open, and JILL YATES is in the kitchen busy preparing toast. JILL is an attractive woman in her early thirties. After a little while she leaves the kitchen, bringing a plate of toast with her. HARRY YATES is sitting facing the table in the recess. He is writing in a notebook. The table is set for tea.

YATES puts down his pen and pushes the notebook to one side. JILL places the toast on the table and sits down.

YATES: Jill, if you murdered someone – if you strangled them with a scarf – what would you do with it?

JILL: With the scarf?

YATES nods.

JILL: I'd get rid of it, I suppose.

YATES: How?

JILL: I don't know. I'd probably burn it.

YATES: (*Nodding*) So would I. So would anyone with intelligence. (*Picking up a piece of toast*) But not this character. Oh, no! He's too smart. He hides it in a violin case where he knows perfectly well it'll be found within a matter of hours.

JILL: Aren't you jumping to conclusions, darling?

YATES: What do you mean?

JILL: It may not be the scarf – if may not be the one you're looking for.

YATES: That's the one all right. I showed it to Marian Hastings. She identified it.

JILL: She could be wrong. She was wrong about the last hat I bought from her.

43

The sound of the front door opening and closing can be heard.

YATES: Yes, well I don't think she's wrong about this.

JILL: Well, here's Jeff, we'll see what that precious Lab of yours has got to say about it.

JEFFREYS enters from the hall. He carries his overcoat over his arm and carries a briefcase.

JEFFREYS: (*To YATES*) Hello, Harry! Jill …

JILL: You look as if you can do with a cup of tea?

JEFFREYS: (*Putting down his coat and briefcase*) Is that really tea? I thought it was a mirage …

(JILL laughs and starts to pour JEFFREYS a cup of tea)

YATES: Never mind the tea. What happened?

JEFFREYS: Harry, I've had a stinker of a day, and I'm so thirsty I could drink …

YATES: (*Impatiently*) What happened?

JEFFREYS: I saw a man called Osborne.

YATES: Little chap – dark glasses – Welsh accent?

JEFFREYS: That's him.

YATES: He's good – been in the Lab for years. Well?

JEFFREYS: (*Opening his brief case and taking out the scarf*) There's no doubt about it, Harry. The murderer used this scarf all right. Osborne found several hairs on it, and a touch of face powder. The hairs belonged to the dead girl.

YATES: Good. Now we're getting somewhere.

(JILL crosses and hands JEFFREYS the cup of tea and a plate of pastries)

44

JILL: Here we are, Jeff.

(*JEFFREYS take the tea, but with a shake of his head refuses the cakes*)

YATES: Well, obviously you spent the morning lounging in the Lab. What happened this afternoon – did you go to the flicks?

JEFFREYS: (*After taking a long drink of tea*) I went to the scarf shop – Briggs and Howland – Bond Street – very exclusive.

YATES: Well?

JEFFREYS: They were not very helpful, I'm afraid. The scarf's Italian, not one of their usual lines. Unfortunately, the assistant who could have helped me is away at the moment. He's got the flu or something. Anyway, I've got his address – he lives quite near.

YATES: Did you ask them about Clifton Morris?

JEFFREYS: Yes, but they were pretty cagey. They think he's a customer of theirs but they're not sure.

YATES: M'm. Well – then what happened?

JEFFREYS: (*After taking another drink of tea*) Well, after that I went down to the Station – Savile Row. (*He takes an envelope out of his pocket and consults it*) Morris first telephoned them on Tuesday evening – that was about the coat, of course, and the valise. Apparently, he's been on the phone several times since then about a cigarette lighter. He seems to think it was in his coat pocket.

YATES: Yes, I know. Has he mentioned the scarf at all?

45

JEFFREYS: No; he doesn't seem concerned about anything except the lighter.

The doorbell rings. YATES looks across at JILL who puts down her cup and goes out into the hall.

JEFFREYS: Are you expecting anyone?

YATES: (*Shaking his head*) No, Jeff. Who did you see at Savile Row?

JEFFREYS: I saw a man called Rowland – awfully nice chap. He's promised to telephone us if the coat turns up.

YATES: Good.

JILL returns.

JILL: (*To YATES*) Harry, Mr Hopedean's here – he wants to see you.

YATES: (*Surprised*) Hopedean?

JEFFREYS: That's the artist chap; the fellow Fay Collins was friendly with.

YATES: Yes …

JILL: He says he wants to see you personally. He'll call back later if necessary. I think I'd see him, Harry. He seems to be in a bit of a flap about something …

YATES: (*Nodding*) All right. (*To JEFFREYS*) Jeff, ask him in.

JEFFREYS nods and goes out into the hall.

YATES: (*To JILL*) Leave us, darling. I'll let you know when he's gone.

JILL nods, moves across to the table, picks up her cup of tea and then crosses towards the kitchen.

JILL: (*To herself, going into the kitchen*) I wish I'd married Bing Crosby. I'll bet he doesn't work on his half day …

JILL closes the kitchen door behind her. JEFFREYS returns with JOHN HOPEDEAN, he is a handsome, faintly

46

artistic looking man, in his early fifties. His clothes are
good, but a shade unconventional.

YATES: Mr Hopedean?

HOPEDEAN: Yes?

YATES: (*Shaking hands*) I'm Detective Inspector
            Yates. (*He indicates JEFFREYS*) This is
            Sergeant Jeffreys.

HOPEDEAN: Yes. (*Nodding to JEFFREYS*) We've met
            before.

YATES: What is it you want to see me about, sir?

HOPEDEAN: (*Taking a letter out of his pocket and
            handing it to YATES*) I thought you might
            like to see this, Inspector.

YATES takes the envelope, opens it and takes out a sheet
of notepaper.

YATES: (*Looking at the notepaper, reading*) "You
            filthy murderer. If you think you can get
            away ..." (*He stops reading, stares at the
            letter, then looks up at HOPEDEAN*) This
            is very unpleasant, sir, to say the least.

HOPEDEAN: (*Tensely*) Yes, and it's not the first one
            I've received. I've had at least half a
            dozen. And telephone calls ... Last
            night a woman rang up – I don't know
            who she was ... My wife answered the
            phone ... (*Shaking his head*) It was just
            the same as that – "Dirty murderer –
            strangler ..." (*Nervously, obviously
            worried*) Inspector, I didn't take much
            notice of it at first, but now it's beginning
            to worry my wife and – well, quite
            frankly, it's getting <u>me</u> down.

JEFFREYS take the letter from YATES and looks at it.

YATES: You say you've received at least half a dozen letters like this?

HOPEDEAN: Yes – probably more.

YATES: Have you got them?

HOPEDEAN: No, I'm afraid I haven't. I was so disgusted I put them on the fire.

YATES: When did this arrive?

HOPEDEAN: This morning. (*To JEFFREYS*) That one happens to be addressed to both my wife and I, so unfortunately …

YATES: (*Interrupting him, with the suggestion of a smile*) Your wife opened it?

HOPEDEAN: (*Nodding*) Yes.

JEFFREYS: (*Looking at the letter and the envelope*) This looks to me like a woman's handwriting. Posted in Hampstead – yesterday afternoon. Have you any idea who's sending these letters, sir?

HOPEDEAN: No, I haven't.

YATES: And didn't you recognise the voice on the telephone?

HOPEDEAN: No, I'm afraid I didn't. She was only on the phone a few seconds.

YATES: I see. (*Pleasantly*) Sit down, sir.

HOPEDEAN hesitates, then sits in the armchair.

YATES: (*Taking the letter back from JEFFREYS*) Well, what exactly would you like me to do about this? Do you want me to try to find out who's sending them?

HOPEDEAN: I don't give a damn who's sending them, I just want them stopped, that's all.

YATES: Well, I'm afraid that isn't going to be very easy. (*He holds up the letter*) But you know, there's nothing very unusual about this sort of thing. You'd be surprised, the number of people who get poison pen letters. I've even had them myself on one occasion.

HOPEDEAN: Yes, I know, but that's not the point … (*He rises; obviously agitated*) These letters don't worry me. They don't worry me personally, but …

YATES: You appear to be very worried, sir.

HOPEDEAN turns towards YATES.

HOPEDEAN: Inspector, I've had one bust-up with my wife over Fay Collins, I don't want another.

JEFFREYS: But Miss Collins is dead, sir, so surely …

YATES: (*Interrupting him*) Just a moment, Jeff. (*To HOPEDEAN*) When did you have this "bust-up", as you call it?

HOPEDEAN: (*Hesitating, wishing he hadn't made the statement*) About a year ago.

YATES: And what happened?

HOPEDEAN: My wife left me.

YATES: Go on …

HOPEDEAN: (*Irritated*) Well, she left me, that's all.

YATES: (*Pleasantly*) She left you because she thought you were having an affair?

HOPEDEAN: Yes, but it wasn't true. Fay and I were friends – very good friends – we had a great deal in common – but we were not having an affair.

YATES: (*With almost charm*) Well, that's all right, sir. We're both men of the world. Your friendship with Miss Collins is no concern

	of ours. But since you're here, sir, there is just one point.
HOPEDEAN:	Well?
YATES:	I think you told Sergeant Jeffreys that the last time you saw Miss Collins was in August of last year?
HOPEDEAN:	Yes, I did.
YATES:	Was that just before she took the flat in Town?
HOPEDEAN:	Yes.
YATES:	In other words, you didn't see Miss Collins – you didn't set eyes on her – once she'd left Littleshaw?
HOPEDEAN:	(*Hesitating*) Yes, that's right, Inspector.
YATES:	(*Pleasantly, but watching HOPEDEAN*) You didn't meet her in Town, for instance?
HOPEDEAN:	No.
YATES:	You never went to the flat?
HOPEDEAN:	No. (*Obviously hesitating*) No, I didn't.
YATES:	I'd like you to be sure about this, sir.
HOPEDEAN:	Well … (*He looks at JEFFREYS, then back. Suddenly:*) Yes, I did. I did see Fay. It was about six weeks ago. I went up to London with some work I'd been doing for a magazine. I had a coffee in one of the coffee bars and just as I was coming out, I bumped into her.
YATES:	Go on, sir.
HOPEDEAN:	She took me back to her flat. We had a few drinks and sat talking for about half an hour.
YATES:	How did she seem? Was she depressed at all?

HOPEDEAN:	No. On the contrary. She was in very good spirits.
YATES:	Go on, sir.
HOPEDEAN:	Well – she suggested we had lunch together, so we arranged to meet at Le Lavencher.
JEFFREYS:	(*Surprised*) Le Lavencher?
HOPEDEAN:	Yes. It's a restaurant in Dover Street. It's quite well known. A lot of the theatre people use it. Anyway, I turned up there at one o'clock and to my surprise there was a message from Fay saying that she couldn't meet me.
JEFFREYS:	Did she say why she couldn't meet you?
HOPEDEAN:	No, she didn't, so I telephoned the flat. There was no reply.
YATES:	I see. Well, thank you, sir. (*A sudden thought*) Oh, Mr Hopedean, I understand from Sergeant Jeffreys that you're an artist …
HOPEDEAN:	(*Nodding*) Yes.
YATES:	You work for magazines and newspapers?
HOPEDEAN:	Yes – pretty well everything I do these days is for a publication of some kind.
YATES:	Well, do you happen to know a man called Clifton Morris?
HOPEDEAN:	(*Surprised*) Clifton Morris?
YATES:	Yes.
HOPEDEAN:	(*With a laugh*) I don't know him. I've heard of him, of course. (*Raising his hand*) He's way up there – one of the hierarchy. I don't mix with those sort of people, Inspector.
YATES:	Did Fay Collins know him?

51

HOPEDEAN: (*Laughing*) No.

YATES: Are you sure?

HOPEDEAN: I'm positive. If she'd met Clifton Morris, we'd have all heard about it.

YATES: (*Closing the interview, holding out his hand*) Well, thank you, Mr Hopedean. (*Indicating the letter he is holding*) And don't worry too much about this sort of thing. You can tell your wife a lot of people have received anonymous letters since Fay Collins was murdered.

HOPEDEAN: (*Taking him literally*) Have they?

YATES: (*Smiling*) You can tell your wife that.

HOPEDEAN: (*Impressed*) Yes … Oh, yes, that's a very good idea. Thank you, Inspector.

HOPEDEAN and YATES cross towards the door.

YATES: There's just one thing, sir …

HOPEDEAN: Yes?

YATES: If you do get any more of these letters, I want to see them – straight away. You understand?

HOPEDEAN: Yes.

YATES: That's important.

HOPEDEAN: (*Nodding*) I understand. (*To JEFFREYS*) Goodbye, Sergeant.

JEFFREYS: Good afternoon, sir.

YATES goes out into the hall with HOPEDEAN. JEFFREYS looks thoughtful and crosses to the table. As he stands and looks at the tea things JILL comes out of the kitchen.

JEFFREYS: (*Turning*) Jill, do you think I could have another cup of tea?

JILL: Yes, of course.

JILL crosses to the table. YATES returns.

52

YATES:	(*To JILL*) I'll have another cup, too, darling.
JILL:	You deserve to have arsenic in yours.
YATES:	(*Moving to the table*) What do you mean?
JILL:	My God, you men! (*Imitating YATES*) Don't worry, old man – we're all men of the world. What's a bit of slap and tickle on the side …
YATES:	(*Laughing*) I didn't say that! In any case, you shouldn't have listened.

The telephone starts to ring.

JILL:	Don't be silly – I always listen!

JILL hands JEFFREYS his cup of tea. YATES smiles and crosses to the telephone.

YATES:	(*On the phone*) Hello? Littleshaw 384.
SHAW:	(*On the other end of the line*) Inspector Yates?
YATES:	Yes.
SHAW:	PC Shaw here, sir. Savile Row …
YATES:	Oh, yes?
SHAW:	Sorry to bother you on your half day, sir.
YATES:	You can say that again!
SHAW:	(*Smiling*) Inspector Rowland asked me to phone you. We've found the coat.
YATES:	Oh, good.
SHAW:	I understand you don't want us to contact Mr Morris until you've seen it.
YATES:	That's right. (*He looks at his watch*) I'll be there about seven-thirty.
SHAW:	Very good, sir. (*He replaces his receiver*)

YATES puts down his receiver and goes back to the table.

YATES:	(*Thoughtfully: To JILL*) I'm sorry, darling – but I've got to go up to Town …

53

JILL: (*Looking at him, serious now*) Yes, all right, Harry. Here's your tea.

YATES joins JILL and JEFFREYS at the tea table.

CUT TO: A Private Office in Savile Row Police Station, London, W1. Night.

ROBERT ROWLAND, a uniformed Police Inspector, is sitting at his desk, writing a letter. He is a pleasant looking man in his early fifties. There is a comfortable armchair with a table with reference books on it, facing the desk. The door opens and a uniformed constable – PC SHAW – enters, carrying a typed memo.

SHAW: (*Putting the memo on the desk*) This has just come in, sir.

ROWLAND: Thank you. (*He reads the memo and looks up*) Hello, what's this about Jackson? ... Is he badly hurt?

SHAW: (*Grinning*) No, sir – only bruised. He chased the man into Hyde Park and fell over a young couple who happened to be ...

ROWLAND: (*Interrupting him*) Yes, all right, Shaw. Let me know when Jackson gets back. I want to see him.

SHAW: Yes, sir. (*Hesitating: then indicating the memo on the desk*) That should interest Inspector Yates, sir.

ROWLAND: (*Looking up*) Why Yates?

SHAW: That's where that girl lived – the one that was murdered. It was her flat the man broke into ...

ROWLAND: (*Looking at the memo again*) 28
                  Welbeck Square … Yes. Yes, you're
                  quite right, it was.

YATES appears in the doorway.

YATES: (*Talking in the open door*) May I come
                  in?

ROWLAND: (*Rising, and coming round his desk*)
                  Inspector Yates?

YATES: Yes.

ROWLAND: (*Shaking hands with him*) I'm Rowland
                  …

YATES: Thank you very much for the phone
                  message. It's kind of you to co-operate
                  like this.

ROWLAND: (*To SHAW*) Fetch the coat.

SHAW: Yes, sir.

SHAW goes out.

ROWLAND: (*Turning towards the desk and picking
                  up the memo*) Yates, I think perhaps
                  this'll interest you even more than the
                  coat. Just over an hour ago a man broke
                  into Fay Collins' flat – 28 Welbeck
                  Square. The alarm was given and one
                  of my men – a chap called Jackson –
                  gave chase.

YATES: What happened?

ROWLAND: I'm afraid Jackson lived up to his
                  reputation. He fell over a courting
                  couple and the man got away.

YATES: Have you got a description of him?

ROWLAND: Yes.

*ROWLAND hands YATES the memo, YATES is looking at
it when SHAW returns carrying a dark double-breasted
overcoat. He puts the coat down on the armchair and goes*

55

*out. YATES finishes reading the memo and then crosses
and picks up the coat. He looks at the name tab at the back
of the collar.*

ROWLAND: Clifton Morris telephoned about twenty
            minutes ago.

YATES: (*Putting down the coat*) Oh – did he?
            (*Anxiously*) What did you say?

ROWLAND: (*Smiling*) Well, fortunately, he didn't
            inquire about the coat. He simply asked if
            we'd found his cigarette lighter.

YATES: It wasn't in the coat, then?

ROWLAND: (*Nodding towards the coat on the
            armchair*) No – there's a pair of gloves,
            but nothing else.

YATES nods and walks back to the armchair.

YATES: (*Touching the collar of the coat*) Where
            did you find it?

ROWLAND: A car attendant brought it in. It was found
            on a bomb site near Ludgate Circus.
            Someone must have dumped it there
            during the night.

YATES: I see. (*He still looks at the coat: after a
            moment*) Rowland, will you do me a
            favour? I'd like to return this coat to
            Morris myself – tonight.

ROWLAND looks at YATES, obviously a little surprised.

ROWLAND: All right. If that's what you want … Go
            ahead.

YATES: (*Pleased and a shade relieved*) Thank you.

The door opens and SHAW returns.

SHAW: (*To ROWLAND*) Jackson's here, sir. He's
            with Dr Thompson.

ROWLAND: I'll come out. (*To YATES*) Don't go – I'll
            be back in a minute.

56

YATES nods and ROWLAND goes out, followed by SHAW. YATES looks slowly round the room, finally glancing across at the door. After a moment he quickly takes the scarf out of his own overcoat pocket and transfers it to the pocket of the coat belonging to CLIFTON MORRIS.

CUT TO: Fulham Road, London, SW. Night.
A 3.4 Jaguar races down the road and brakes to a standstill opposite a telephone box on the corner of the street. ERIC jumps out of the car and runs into a telephone box.

CUT TO: Inside the telephone box on the Fulham Road. Night.
ERIC is dialling a number. He looks worried, excited, and faintly dishevelled.

CUT TO: The Drawing room of CLIFTON MORRIS' Flat. Night.
For the duration of this conversation, we cut back and forth between MORRIS and ERIC.

CLIFTON MORRIS is anxiously pacing up and down the room. He looks distinctly worried. There is a whisky and soda in his hand, and he is smoking a cigar. He wears part of a dark suit, and a smoking jacket. He crosses to the drinks table and is about to strengthen his drink with another shot of whisky when the telephone rings. He puts down the drink and quickly crosses to the telephone.
MORRIS: (*Picking up the receiver*) Hello …
ERIC presses button A.
ERIC: Mr Morris …?
MORRIS: Yes.
ERIC: This is Eric …

57

MORRIS: Eric, where are you? What happened?

ERIC: I'm in a call box on the Fulham Road.

MORRIS: (*Irritated*) What on earth are you doing there?

ERIC: (*Nervously*) A policeman spotted me coming out of the flat. I had to make a dash for it.

MORRIS: Oh, my God! Did he see you? Are you all right, Eric?

ERIC: (*With a little laugh*) Yes, he saw me, but fortunately I managed to give him the slip. It was a very near thing, though.

MORRIS: Did you get …

ERIC: No, I didn't. It's not there. It's not in the flat.

MORRIS: Are you sure?

ERIC: Yes, I'm absolutely sure. I went through every drawer and cupboard in the place. If you ask me, you left it too late.

MORRIS: (*Thoughtfully*) Yes, it rather looks like it. (*Suddenly*) All right, Eric. Which car have you got?

ERIC: The Jaguar.

MORRIS: Go down to Angmering. Stay there till you hear from me.

MORRIS thoughtfully replaces the receiver and as he does so the doorbell rings. He looks towards the hall.

CUT TO: Outside the front door of the flat. Night.

YATES is standing in the carpeted corridor facing the door, the overcoat is over his arm. The door is opened, and YATES finds himself facing CLIFTON MORRIS.

YATES: Good evening, sir.

MORRIS: (*Surprised*) Oh, hello, Inspector.

YATES: (*Pleasantly*) We've found your coat, Mr Morris. May I come in, sir?

MORRIS: Yes, of course.

58

YATES goes into the entrance hall. MORRIS closes the door.

YATES:　A car attendant found it on a bomb site near Ludgate Circus.

MORRIS: (*Taking the coat from YATES*) Good heavens above, how on earth did it get there, Inspector?

CUT TO:　The drawing room.

(*MORRIS enters, carrying the coat, followed by YATES*)

YATES:　I'm afraid the lighter's still missing, sir.

MORRIS:　Oh, damn!

MORRIS puts the coat down on a chair: he takes the scarf and gloves from a pocket.

YATES:　Have you got a description of it?

MORRIS: Yes. (*Showing the size of the lighter with his fingers*) It's about that big, nine carat gold – with a Regimental Crest on it.

YATES:　Well, it might turn up. You've been lucky so far, with the coat and the valise.

MORRIS:　Yes, I suppose I have.

YATES:　(*Casually*) Is your man off tonight?

MORRIS: (*Passing it off*) Yes. He's gone up to Scotland for two or three days. Left yesterday … Can I get you a drink, Inspector?

YATES:　No, I don't think so, thank you very much. (*Pointing to the coat*) It is your coat, of course, sir?

MORRIS: (*Looking at the coat*) Oh, yes. Yes, this is it all right.

YATES:　And the scarf?

MORRIS: (*Picking up the scarf*) Yes, this is my … (*A sudden realisation*) Oh, yes, you wanted to see this, didn't you?

59

YATES: (*Pointing to the scarf in MORRIS' hand*) Is that
                your scarf, sir?

MORRIS looks at the scarf, then at YATES.

MORRIS: Yes.

YATES: You're quite sure?

MORRIS: (*Looking at the scarf again*) Why, yes …

*YATES looks at MORRIS for a moment and then takes the
scarf out of his hand.*

YATES: I think there's something you ought to know
                about this scarf, Mr Morris. In the first place
                we didn't find it in the overcoat and in the
                second place…

MORRIS: (*Interrupting him*) Well, where did you find it?

YATES: In a violin case belonging to a young man
                called Gerald Quincey.

MORRIS: In a violin … (*With a laugh*) You're joking …

YATES: No, sir – I'm not joking. (*Holding up the scarf*)
                I sent it to Scotland Yard – to the Lab. (*After a
                moment*) Fay Collins was strangled. She was
                strangled with this scarf, Mr Morris.

MORRIS looks at YATES and moves towards him.

MORRIS: (*Quietly, yet annoyed*) Then you put that scarf
                in the overcoat pocket …

YATES: (*Unperturbed*) Yes.

MORRIS: … And deliberately tricked me into saying it
                was mine?

YATES: Tricked you, sir? It's either your scarf or it
                isn't. I simply asked you to identify it.

MORRIS: (*Annoyed*) Supposing someone brought you
                your overcoat and you found a scarf in the
                pocket. A scarf which looked exactly like the
                one you'd lost …

YATES: Well?

MORRIS: Wouldn't you jump to the conclusion it was yours?

YATES: (*Evasively, with the suggestion of a smile*) I try awfully hard not to jump to conclusions, sir.

MORRIS: Well, if you ask me, I don't think you try hard enough!

YATES: What does that mean, exactly?

MORRIS: (*After a moment, facing YATES*) You think I murdered Fay Collins, don't you?

YATES: This is your scarf, sir, and it's been proved …

MORRIS: (*Interrupting him*) It's not my scarf! I made a mistake! (*Turning away*) This is quite ridiculous! I didn't even know Fay Collins. I wasn't anywhere near Littleshaw the night she was murdered.

YATES: (*Quietly*) It's a pity you can't prove that, sir.

MORRIS: (*Turning, slowly*) Well – perhaps I can. Ever since your last visit I've tried to remember what actually happened that night. I've tried to recall details; apparently unimportant things …

YATES: Well?

MORRIS: Well, this morning I suddenly remembered something …

YATES: Go on …

MORRIS: I went to the cinema the night Fay Collins was murdered – the one in Curzon Street.

YATES: Yes, you told me.

MORRIS: I left about a quarter past ten. Just as I was getting into a taxi a girl came out of the cinema. I didn't take much notice of her, although I realise now, I vaguely recognised her at the time.

YATES: Did she recognise you, Mr Morris?

MORRIS: (*Quietly, nodding*) Yes, I think she did.

YATES: Who was this girl?

MORRIS: Her name's Winston – Diana Winston. She's a journalist.

YATES: Does she work for you?

MORRIS: No, she's a freelance – or she was. She did some articles for a magazine of mine several years ago. They weren't very good, I'm afraid.

YATES: Have you got in touch with Miss Winston?

MORRIS: Good heavens, no, I've just told you – I only remembered this incident this morning.

YATES: Well, if I were you, I would, sir. I'd make a point of it – straight away.

YATES folds up the scarf and puts it into his own overcoat pocket.

MORRIS: Yes, all right, Inspector.

YATES: (*As he puts the scarf away*) How long have you known Miss Weston?

MORRIS: I don't actually know her. I met her once – at a party – about five years ago.

YATES: Five years ago? You obviously have a very good memory for faces, sir.

MORRIS: Yes, I have, as a matter of fact.

YATES: Well – let's hope Miss Winston shares your talent in that direction. (*Smiling, with a nod*) Goodnight, Mr Morris.

MORRIS: Goodnight, Inspector.

YATES walks out into the hall followed by CLIFTON MORRIS. After a moment, MORRIS returns: he looks thoughtful. He hesitates for a moment, then suddenly looks at his watch and crosses towards the telephone. He picks up the receiver and dials a number. There is a pause – then we hear the number ringing out.

NORMAN: (*A cultured, top executive voice, on the other end of the line*) Hyde Park 3183 …

MORRIS: Norman? … Morris here …

NORMAN: Oh, good evening, sir. I was just going to phone you. I've been in touch with Montreal about the syndication problem and they feel …

MORRIS: (*Interrupting him*) Norman, I don't want to talk about the syndication. Do you remember a girl called Diana Winston?

NORMAN: (*Faintly surprised*) Yes, I do.

MORRIS: I want to see her. Arrange for her to be in my office tomorrow morning. Any time after ten o'clock.

NORMAN: Well – do you think we could make it sometime in the afternoon?

MORRIS: (*Annoyed*) Why the afternoon?

NORMAN: I've got to contact her, sir, and she's got to get here.

MORRIS: Get here – what do you mean?

NORMAN: She's in Paris. She works for the Flaubert people.

MORRIS: (*Stunned*) In Paris?

NORMAN: Yes.

MORRIS: (*Tensely*) How long has she been in Paris?

NORMAN: Oh – about eighteen months, I should say.

MORRIS: (*Quietly*) All right, Norman. Forget it.

MORRIS replaces the receiver and stands by the table, hand on the telephone. He looks thoughtful and distinctly worried. After a little while he turns away from the table and as he does so the telephone rings. He looks at it for a moment, undecided whether to answer it or not, then he picks up the receiver.

MORRIS: (*On the phone*) Hello?

KIM: (*On the other end of the line*) Mr Morris?

MORRIS: Who is that?

KIM:	Is that Clifton Morris?
MORRIS:	(*After a momentary hesitation, abruptly*) Yes, it is. Who is what? What is it you want?
KIM:	(*Quietly*) Are you still interested in the letter, Mr Morris?
MORRIS:	What letter?
KIM:	The one you tried to get this afternoon.
MORRIS:	(*Hesitating, then indignantly*) I don't know what you're talking about. What the devil is this? Who are you?
KIM:	If you don't know what I'm talking about, Sweetie, there's no point in my telling you who I am. Goodbye …
MORRIS:	(*Quickly, stopping her*) No, wait a moment! Don't ring off … (*Softly: curious*) Who are you?
KIM:	Fay Collins was a friend of mine.
MORRIS:	Oh. Oh, I see … (*Nervously*) Well, what is it you want?
KIM:	It's not what I want, Sweetie. It's what you want. Do you know The Take-Off?
MORRIS:	The Take-Off? No – what's that?
KIM:	It's a club in Helston Street. I'm surprised you don't know it, Mr Morris, a big businessman like you. Drop in one night, Honey – tonight if you like.
MORRIS:	(*Tensely*) Who are you?
KIM:	… Just ask for Kim … (*She replaces the receiver*)

MORRIS stands thoughtfully.

CUT TO: A flashing sign advertising "The Take-Off" a Variety (Strip-Tease) Club for World Weary Business

Men. The sign shows a typical showgirl waving a very large Prince of Wales fan.

CUT TO: A corridor in The Take-Off Club with dressing rooms on either side.

Several showgirls in various non-committal costumes pass to and fro along the corridor. HECTOR, a middle-aged call boy, is also present – knocking on various doors, telling the girls to "Hurry along, please!", "Come along, now", "Ducky for goodness sake …". In the near background from the stage can be heard music and dancing, and a certain amount of laughter.

KIM STEVENS comes down the corridor and goes to one of the dressing rooms. Her costume – what there is of it – suggests that she is the star of the show.

CUT TO: KIM STEVENS' Dressing Room at The Take-Off Club.

This is a room with make-up table, stool, armchair, dilapidated chest of drawers etc. Bottles stand on the chest of drawers, and also on a table with it at right angles to a large screen. This screen conceals a corner of the room and is used as a private changing room. A brand-new tape recorder stands open on the table. Framed photographs of show people – past and present – line the walls.

KIM is sitting at the make-up table, painting her lips when there is a knock on the door and HECTOR pops his head in.

HECTOR: You've got a visitor!

KIM rises as CLIFTON MORRIS comes into the dressing room.

MORRIS: (*Hesitantly*) Kim?

65

KIM: Yes. Hello, Sweetie.

MORRIS: (*Stiffly*) Good evening.

KIM looks at him and gives a little smile. They stand looking at each other for a moment, MORRIS obviously a little taken aback by her appearance. KIM crosses towards the chest of drawers.

KIM: Take a pew.

MORRIS hesitates, then sits on the arm of the armchair.

KIM: Do you want a drink?

MORRIS: No.

KIM: Okay.

KIM mixes herself a gin and tonic. MORRIS looks round the room, then at KIM – he is faintly embarrassed by the situation and his surroundings.

MORRIS: (*Clearing his throat*) Miss Stevens, I haven't a lot of time, so I'd be very grateful if …

KIM: (*Turning towards him, interrupting*) Haven't you, Honey?

MORRIS: No. I'm a very busy man. (*He glances at his wristlet watch*) I've got another appointment at half past seven.

KIM gives a little smile and crosses to the stool at the make-up table.

KIM: Relax, Sweetie … Take it easy … (*She drinks her gin and tonic, looking at him over the top of the glass*) Have you seen the show?

MORRIS: No.

KIM: You should. Drop in one afternoon. You'd enjoy it.

MORRIS: (*Frigidly*) I'm not very interested in the theatre.

KIM: This isn't the Theatre, Sweetie. You'd feel at home here. There's quite a board meeting some afternoons. Memos and everything.

MORRIS: (*Slowly; hesitant*) … You said something about
a letter …

KIM: That's right.

MORRIS: Which letter were you referring to?

KIM: Don't you know?

MORRIS: (*Hesitantly*) No.

KIM: Then why did you come?

MORRIS: I – I was curious.

KIM: (*Laughing*) Curious? You sound like one of
our regulars.

MORRIS: (*After a moment*) Was Fay Collins a friend of
yours?

KIM: She certainly was. A very good friend. Was she
a friend of yours too, Sweetie?

MORRIS: No.

KIM: (*Examining her make-up in the mirror*) Then
why did you telephone her – and write her a
letter? A nice, chummy little letter …

MORRIS: (*Rising, puzzled*) How did you know I
telephoned her?

KIM: (*Smiling*) You did, didn't you?

MORRIS: (*Still puzzled*) Yes, but only once – from a call
box.

KIM: That's right, Honey. From a call box.

*KIM looks at MORRIS for a moment, then turns and
switches on the tape recorder. MORRIS stares in
amazement, first at KIM, then at the tape recorder on the
table. The tape revolves.*

MORRIS: (*Pointing to the recorder*) What is this?

KIM: It's a tape recorder.

MORRIS: Yes, I know that, but …

*A noise can be heard on the tape recorder. The noise of a
number ringing out on a telephone exchange. We hear a
telephone receiver being lifted – the distant noise of coins*

dropping into a box – and then the voices of FAY COLLINS and CLIFTON MORRIS. The recording has obviously been taken in FAY's flat. MORRIS is on the other end of the line. During the following tape-recording sequence KIM is smiling and faintly amused whilst MORRIS looks worried and bewildered as he stares at the tape recorder.

FAY: Hello?

MORRIS: (*Tensely*) Fay? This is Terry …

FAY: (*Agitated*) What is it? What is it you want?

MORRIS: (*Still tense*) I got your message this morning.

FAY: I don't want to discuss it. I told you – I don't want to talk about it on the telephone.

MORRIS: (*Desperately, pleading*) Fay, listen – please don't ring off! I've changed my mind.

FAY: I don't believe you.

MORRIS: It's true. It's true, Fay. I've written you a letter. You'll get it tomorrow morning.

FAY: (*After a moment*) Well –?

MORRIS: I'll meet you – I'll meet you anywhere you like. Honestly, darling.

FAY: (*After a moment, unemotional, almost business like*) All right. Littleshaw. Wednesday next. On the corner of Layton Avenue. Nine o'clock …

MORRIS: (*Softly, resigned*) I'll be there, Fay.

We hear FAY's receiver being replaced. KIM reaches out and stops the recorder. MORRIS, standing at the recorder, looks up at KIM.

KIM: That's not the only tape – there's another one, much clearer than that …

AS KIM speaks the door is thrown open and HECTOR pops his head into the room.

HECTOR: (*To KIM*) Three minutes, Kim!

KIM: Okay, Hector.

The door closes. There is a pause. MORRIS continues to look at KIM, then he looks down at the recorder again.

MORRIS: (*After a moment, not looking at KIM*) Have you got that letter?

KIM: No. But I can get it.

MORRIS: (*Looking up*) For how much?

KIM smiles and rises from the stool.

KIM: Now you're really interested, aren't you? (*She walks past MORRIS and opens the door*) I'll get in touch – I'll send you a telegram, Sweetie.

KIM goes out and the door closes.

CUT TO: YATES' Office at Littleshaw Police Station. The Following Morning.

YATES is sitting at his desk, reading a report. PC KENT enters with a folder which he puts down on the desk in front of YATES.

YATES: Has Mr Matthews arrived?

KENT: Not yet, sir, but Mr Goodman would like to see you.

YATES: Goodman? What's he want?

KENT: I don't know, sir. He didn't say.

YATES: All right, show him in.

KENT turns towards the door, then hesitates. YATES looks up at him.

KENT: Inspector …

YATES: Yes?

KENT: The missis and I dropped into the Fox and Goose last night.

YATES: Well?

KENT: Mr Collins was there. He wasn't half shooting his mouth off.

YATES: What about?

69

KENT: He said the police were doing nothing
                about his sister's murder – just taking it
                easy, sitting on   their backsides.
YATES: Did you disillusion him, Kent?
KENT: No, sir. He was a bit tight and – well, the
                wife told me to keep out of it.

YATES gives a nod of approval.

YATES: (*Quietly*) I'll see Goodman.
KENT: Yes, sir.

*KENT goes out. YATES rises and comes round the desk.
He stands for a moment, deep in thought, obviously
thinking of EDWARD COLLINS. KENT shows in
ALISTAIR GOODMAN. GOODMAN is wearing the same
clothes as in episode one.*

YATES: (*Looking   up*) Good   morning,   Mr
                Goodman. Come along in, sir.
GOODMAN: Sorry to bother you, Inspector. Pig of a
                morning.
YATES: Yes, it is. (*HE returns to his desk and
                indicates the armchair to GOODMAN*) Sit
                down, sir.
GOODMAN: Oh, thank you. (*He sits in the armchair*)
YATES: What can I do for you, Mr Goodman?
GOODMAN: One of my chaps – fellow called Kelsey –
                went up to the Four Acre this morning.
                That's the field where Miss Collins …
YATES: (Nodding) Yes, I know.
GOODMAN: Well, to cut a long story short, I told old
                Kelsey to plough the bottom half of the
                field – that's the bit near the meadow.
                Ruddy hard going. Hate the job myself.
                Well, about an hour ago the fool ran out of
                paraffin and had to walk back to the farm
                …

70

YATES: Go on …

GOODMAN: Well, to cut a long story short, Inspector …

YATES: (*Impatiently*) Don't bother to cut it short, sir. Just give me the details …

GOODMAN: What? Oh, yes! (*With a laugh*) Yes! I see what you mean … (*He puts his hand in his jacket pocket*) Well … (*Amused*) I've got to say it. To cut a long story short, old Kelsey found this thing – near the ditch – not far from where your chap found the handbag …

GOODMAN takes his hand out of his pocket and produces a gold, square shaped cigarette lighter with a Regimental Crest on it.

END OF EPISODE TWO

EPISODE THREE

OPEN TO: YATES' Office at Littleshaw Police Station. Day.

YATES rises from the desk and joins GOODMAN.

YATES: (*Taking the lighter out of GOODMAN's hand*) Where did you say this was found?

GOODMAN: Near the ditch – not far from where your man Jeffreys found the handbag.

YATES: (*After a moment; examining the lighter*) Who actually found it?

GOODMAN: (*Rising*) Old Kelsey … You know him, Inspector. Wizened-up little fellow; always wears a beret.

YATES: Oh, yes … Yes, I know the chap you mean.

GOODMAN: (*Pointing to the lighter*) What is that – a Regimental Crest, or something?

YATES: I should imagine so. (*Suddenly, holding out his hand, dismissing him*) Well, thank you Mr Goodman.

JEFFREYS enters. He is surprised to see GOODMAN.

JEFFREYS: (*To YATES*) Oh, I'm sorry, sir, I thought you were alone.

YATES: That's all right. Come in, Jeff. Mr Goodman's just leaving.

GOODMAN: Hello, sergeant …

JEFFREYS: Good morning, sir …

GOODMAN: (*To YATES*) Goodbye, Inspector.

YATES: Goodbye, Mr Goodman – and thank you very much.

GOODMAN goes out. YATES closes the door.

JEFFREYS: You know, I'm damned if I can see what Marian Hastings sees in that chap. He's years older than she is.

YATES: (*Crossing to the desk*) … And worth pots of money.

JEFFREYS: Is he worth pots of money?

YATES: Well, they say so. He owns Kingsbury Farm and he's got three or four hundred acres on the other side of town. (*He picks up the lighter*) He brought this – an old boy called Kelsey found it.

JEFFREYS: (*Taking the lighter – surprised*) Where?

YATES: In the field; near where you found the handbag.

JEFFREYS: But surely this is the one Morris lost – the one that was in the overcoat.

YATES: Yes, if it ever was in the overcoat. (*Taking the lighter from JEFFREYS and putting it down on the desk*) What happened this morning? Did you see that young fellow from the scarf shop?

JEFFREYS: Yes. I spent half an hour with him. He lives at Oakfield.

YATES: Well?

JEFFREYS takes the scarf out of his coat pocket and puts it down on the desk.

JEFFREYS: He remembers selling that scarf, or one exactly like it, to Fay Collins – just over three weeks ago.

YATES: Three weeks ago?

JEFFREYS: Yes, about six days before the murder. That ties up with the letter, doesn't it.

YATES: Yes, it could do …

JEFFREYS: So once we can prove that Morris sent the letter …

YATES: Wait a minute! Not so fast … This chap – what's his name? …

JEFFREYS: Ripley …
YATES: Ripley must have sold quite a few of these
             scarves at one time or another. How come
             he remembers Fay Collins?
JEFFREYS: I showed him a photograph of her.
YATES: And he recognised her?
JEFFREYS: Yes; but he remembered her, Harry, apart
             from the photograph. Apparently, Fay
             couldn't make up her mind about the scarf.
             She told him it was a present for a friend
             of hers – an extremely wealthy man who
             was difficult to please (*He is faintly
             amused*) Ripley says she kept changing
             her mind the whole time. I gather she very
             nearly finished up with a smoking jacket.
YATES: (*Looking at JEFFREYS, curious*) A
             smoking jacket …
JEFFREYS: (*Still amused*) Yes …

*YATES rises; he appears rather pleased with something
JEFFREYS has said. He picks up the scarf and places it in
a drawer.*

YATES: (*Locking the drawer*) Thank you, Jeff.
             You've done very well.

*JEFFREYS looks at YATES, faintly puzzled. The door
opens and the REVEREND MATTHEWS can be see
standing in the doorway, behind PC KENT.*

KENT: Mr Matthews, sir.
YATES: Oh, good morning, sir. Come along in, Mr
             Matthews. (*To JEFFREYS*) I'll see you
             later.
MATTHEWS: Good morning, Sergeant.
JEFFREYS: Hello, vicar. I trust you're keeping well,
             sir?

77

MATTHEWS: Yes, thank the Lord, I'm very well. And you, Sergeant?

JEFFREYS: (*Going out*) Oh, I'm all right, sir, thank you.

YATES: (*Indicating a chair*) Sit down, Padre.

MATTHEWS sits in the chair. YATES picks up a box and offers him a cigarette. The vicar shakes his head. As he replaces the box, MATTHEWS notices the lighter on the table. He looks at it but makes no comment. YATES notices the look but says nothing; he sits on the edge of the desk facing MATTHEWS.

MATTHEWS: You must be a very busy man these days, Inspector?

YATES: Yes, I am.

MATTHEWS: Which makes me all the more curious.

YATES: Curious?

MATTHEWS: Yes. I'm wondering why you sent for me.

YATES: (*Facing MATTHEWS*) Padre, I understand you know a man called Clifton Morris?

MATTHEWS: Terry Morris? Yes, I do. I do indeed.

YATES: His name isn't Terry, sir. It's Clifton.

MATTHEWS: Yes, I know. (*Smiling*) Which is why, I imagine, he prefers to be called Terry. (*A shrug*) Whether his family call him Terry or not, I wouldn't know. We certainly called him that at Cambridge.

YATES: Is he a close friend of yours?

MATTHEWS: No, I wouldn't call him a close friend, exactly. He's a man I like and admire.

YATES: Why do you admire him, sir?

MATTHEWS: Well, Terry didn't do very well at Cambridge, you know, and he didn't exactly set the Thames on fire during the war. Then, suddenly, I think it was in 1946

78

	– he borrowed two hundred pounds from somebody and started a magazine. Everyone laughed at him. He was a joke in Fleet Street – nothing more or less than a joke. Well, they're not laughing at him now, are they?
YATES:	No. No, they're certainly not. Is he a millionaire?
MATTHEWS:	Well, they say so. He's certainly a very wealthy man.
YATES:	When did you first meet him?
MATTHEWS:	(*Thoughtfully*) About 1938 … Yes '38 … I knew his brother quite well – Wrenson …
YATES:	Wrenson? …
MATTHEWS:	Yes, a very different type from Terry, although curiously enough they were devoted to each other. Wrenson … Isn't that an extraordinary Christian name? Wrenson and Clifton … I really can't imagine why their parents chose such outlandish names. (*Suddenly, as if the thought had just occurred to him*) But tell me – why are you interested in Terry?

YATES looks at MATTHEWS for a moment and then returns to his position behind the desk.

YATES:	(*Quietly, examining a ruler*) Well, confidentially, Padre – we think he may have had something to do with the Collins murder.
MATTHEWS:	(*Staggered*) No! No, surely not …
YATES:	(*Nodding*) We believe he met Miss Collins the night she was murdered.
MATTHEWS:	What does Terry say about this? Have you spoken to him?

YATES: Yes. He claims he was at a cinema on the night in question. He says a girl called Diana Winston will corroborate his story. Unfortunately, she hasn't – not yet, at any rate.

MATTHEWS: But who told you about Terry, in the first place?

YATES: (*After a momentary hesitation*) Miss Hastings did. She saw a photograph of him a couple of days ago and identified him as the man who was with Fay Collins.

MATTHEWS: Oh, I see.

YATES: Of course, she gave us a description of the man the day she got back from the Continent, but unfortunately, we were unable to …

MATTHEWS: (*Interrupting him*) From the Continent?

YATES: Yes.

MATTHEWS: (*Looking at YATES; puzzled*) When was Miss Hastings on the Continent, then?

YATES: She flew to Geneva the morning after the murder was committed.

MATTHEWS: (*Puzzled*) I'm afraid I don't quite follow you, Inspector. I thought the murder was committed on the night of January the 7th?

YATES: It was. Wednesday, January 7th.

MATTHEWS: And you say Miss Hastings flew to Geneva the next morning?

YATES: Yes.

MATTHEWS: And when did she get back?

YATES: She came back the moment she read about the murder. I think it was six days later – the 12th or 13th – I'm not sure.

MATTHEWS: But you know, this is extraordinary! Really quite extraordinary …

YATES: (*Rising, coming round the desk*) What do you mean?

MATTHEWS: Miss Hastings was in London on the Friday morning … Friday, January 9th …

YATES: But she couldn't have been!

MATTHEWS: She was. I saw her getting into a taxi in Regent Street.

YATES: (*Puzzled*) Did she see you?

MATTHEWS: No.

YATES: You're sure it was Miss Hastings?

MATTHEWS: (*Emphatically*) I'm positive.

YATES: And you're sure of the date?

MATTHEWS: I'm absolutely sure. Friday, January the 9th.

YATES looks at MATTHEWS, puzzled and worried.

MATTHEWS: Don't you believe me, Inspector?

CUT TO: The Drawing Room of CLIFTON MORRIS' flat in London. Evening.

The cigarette lighter is in a man's hand. The hand flicks the lighter and the flame is raised to a cigarette in a man's mouth. The camera slowly tracks back to reveal MORRIS holding the lighter and standing with his back to the fireplace. He wears a dinner jacket. His overcoat, evening scarf, and hat are on the settee.

MORRIS: … Yes, this is mine, Inspector, there's no doubt about it. I'm very grateful to you. Thank you very much. (*He looks at the lighter*) I should hate to have lost it. My C.O. gave it to me during the war.

YATES is stood facing MORRIS.

81

YATES: In case you're interested, sir, it was found in a field in Littleshaw.

MORRIS: (*Puzzled*) Littleshaw?

YATES: Yes. About twenty yards from where Fay Collins was murdered.

MORRIS crosses and sits on the settee; he looks at the lighter in his hand. A pause.

MORRIS: Then I suppose you think I lied? I suppose you think I lost it when the murder was committed?

YATES: (*Quite simply*) Did you?

MORRIS: (*Shaking his head, emphatically*) No …

YATES sits on the arm of the chair; leans forward towards MORRIS.

YATES: Mr Morris, you remember that scarf I showed you the other day?

MORRIS: Yes.

YATES: Well, assuming it isn't yours, then you must have one exactly like it.

MORRIS: Yes, I have. It's still missing.

YARES: Where did you buy if from, sir?

MORRIS: From a shop in Bond Street. Briggs and Howland I think it's called.

YATES: When?

MORRIS: About a year or so ago. I bought two.

YATES: (*Surprised*) Two?

MORRIS: Yes. The one that's missing and a white one. (*He picks up the dress scarf from the settee*) This – for evening wear.

YATES: (*Nodding*) Oh, I see. Miss Collins bought a scarf from Briggs and Howland. (*Indicating the scarf on the settee*) Not like this – like the other one. She bought it for a friend of hers.

82

MORRIS: Well?

YATES: (*Taking the telegram out of his pocket*) She sent her friend the scarf and he acknowledged it with this telegram. (*He looks at MORRIS*) Would you like to know what it says, Mr Morris?

MORRIS doesn't reply: YATES looks at him, then reads the telegram.

YATES: "Many thanks for scarf. Love. Terry."

YATES looks up at MORRIS, who still makes no comment.

YATES: You don't seem very surprised, sir? Does that mean you sent this?

MORRIS: No; it simply means I'm becoming immune to your surprises, Inspector.

YATES: (*Quietly*) Did you send this telegram?

MORRIS: Of course I didn't! And for a very good reason …

YATES: Well?

MORRIS: She didn't send me the scarf!

YATES: I see. Well, thank you very much, sir. *(Putting the telegram into his pocket)* Oh, Mr Morris, do you happen to know a restaurant called Le Lava … Now what the devil is it?

MORRIS: Le Lavencher?

YATES: That's it.

MORRIS: Yes, I do. I go there quite often.

YATES: So did Miss Collins.

MORRIS: Quite a lot of people go to Le Lavencher, Inspector. It's a popular restaurant.

YATES: What's it called, sir? Le Lav …

MORRIS: Le Lavencher.

YATES: (*Taking a ball pen and an envelope from his pocket*) Le Lav – en – cher …

YATES starts to write the name on the envelope, then gives a little laugh, and offers MORRIS the pen and envelope.

YATES: Would you mind jotting it down for me? French was never my strong point, I'm afraid.

MORRIS hesitates a flicker of a second, and then takes the pen and envelope. He writes the name down and then returns the pen and envelope to YATES.

YATES: Thank you.

MORRIS: Now, Inspector, you've been asking me quite a lot of questions during the past twenty-four-hours; do you think I might ask you one for a change?

YATES: (*Looking at the writing on the envelope*) Yes, of course. (*He puts the envelope in his pocket*) Go ahead.

MORRIS: Why haven't you arrested me? You obviously think I murdered Fay Collins. With the information you've got you could get a warrant out for me, just like that! (*He snaps his fingers*)

YATES: Twelve months ago, when I was attached to Scotland Yard, I took a warrant out for someone – just like that! (*He snaps his fingers*) I made a mistake. I don't want to make another one if I can help it. (*Smiling*) Any more questions, Mr Morris?

MORRIS: (*Shaking his head*) No.

YATES: Then I'll say goodnight. It's all right, sir, I can see myself out. (*He crosses towards the hall, then hesitates*) Oh – I take it you haven't found that girl yet – the one that was at the cinema? Diana – what's her name?

MORRIS: Diana Winston. No – no, I'm afraid I haven't.

YATES: (*Quietly, with a little nod*) I should certainly try to find her, sir, if I were you. (*He turns and goes out*)

MORRIS crosses towards the hall, waits a moment, then as the front door is heard closing, he returns to the settee. He looks thoughtful and worried. He glances at his wristlet watch, and then picks up the coat and scarf and puts them on. He is tying the scarf when the telephone rings. He moves to the table and picks up the receiver.

MORRIS: (*On the phone*) Hello? …

NORMAN: (*On the other end of the line*) Norman here, sir.

MORRIS: Oh, hello, Norman …

NORMAN: I've been in touch with the Accountants, sir. The figures are in the post – you'll get them tomorrow morning.

MORRIS: Thank you, Norman. Goodbye …

NORMAN: (*Stopping him*) Just a moment! You know that girl you mentioned, sir?

MORRIS: (*Impatiently*) Girl? No …

NORMAN: You remember – you asked me about a girl called Diana Winston.

MORRIS: (*Suddenly*) Oh, yes! Yes, of course!

NORMAN: Well, I'm most frightfully sorry, sir. I made a mistake. She's not in Paris. The Flaubert people got rid of her over a year ago.

MORRIS: Well, where is she now?

NORMAN: She's back in London, doing freelance work.

MORRIS: (*Quickly*) Norman, listen – phone her straight away and ask her to come …

NORMAN: (*Interrupting him*) I've already done so.
            She's calling in the office tomorrow
            afternoon.
MORRIS: Well, immediately she arrives, put her in a
            cab and bring her round here – to the flat –
            you understand?
NORMAN: (*Puzzled*) Yes. Yes, very good, sir.
MORRIS: Thank you, Norman.
*MORRIS smiles to himself and slowly replaces the
receiver.*

CUT TO: YATES' Office at Littleshaw Police Station.
Morning.

*MARIAN HASTINGS is sat facing the desk and
DETECTIVE INSPECTOR YATES. She wears a fur stole
and looks puzzled, but quite self-possessed. YATES has a
pencil in his hand and a desk diary in front of him.*
YATES: (*Not looking up*) … You still haven't
            answered my question, Miss Hastings.
MARIAN: For the simple reason that I don't
            understand it.
YATES: (*Looking up, smiling at her*) I'm asking
            you to account for your movements
            between January 7th and January 13th of
            this year.
MARIAN: But why on earth should I do that?
            Besides, you know where I was on
            January the 7th. That was the night I saw
            Fay Collins.
YATES: (*Looking down at the diary*) And January
            the 8th …?
MARIAN: (*Irritated*) I told you. I went to Geneva and
            then on to Chamonix.

86

YATES: (*Looking at her*) Where did you stay in Chamonix?

MARIAN: At a hotel called Le Petit Boheme.

YATES: (*Quietly; writing the name on a paid*) Le Petit Boheme … Thank you.

MARIAN: (*Puzzled, watching YATES*) Avenue de Gaulle, since you're interested …

YATES: (*Smiling, writing the address down*) Thank you, Miss Hastings. Now I want to make sure I've got this right. (*He looks at the diary again*) You left Littleshaw on the night of Wednesday, January the 7th. You stayed the night in London and flew to Geneva next morning – Thursday, January the 8th …

MARIAN: (*With a little smile*) No.

YATES: (*Looking up*) No?

MARIAN: (*Shaking her head*) No. I left for Geneva on the Thursday morning, but I didn't fly. I travelled by train.

YATES: But surely, the first time you came here you told me you flew?

MARIAN: No, you're mistaken. I went by train. I simply loathe flying. I never fly anywhere if I can help it.

YATES: I see. (*Looking at the diary again*) Then, you arrived in Geneva on Friday, January the 9th …

MARIAN: That's right. A friend of mine met me at Chamonix. We got there about half-past four in the afternoon.

YATES looks at Marian; he closes the diary and rises and comes round the desk.

YATES: Miss Hastings, what would you say if I told you a friend of mine saw you in London on the Friday morning – Friday, January the 9th?

MARIAN: (*Irritated*) I should say your friend was either round the bend or needed spectacles. (*She rises*) Probably both. (*Pulling her stole onto her shoulders*) Anyway, you can soon find out if I'm telling the truth. (*Indicates the pad on the desk*) Write to the hotel.

YATES: (*Nodding politely*) Thank you, Miss Hastings.

MARIAN: (*Suddenly annoyed*) In any case, you know, I don't really see what business it is of yours what I was doing on Friday, January the 9th or 10th, or whatever it was …

YATES: (*Smiling*) The 9th …

MARIAN: Very well, the 9th. Supposing I was in London?

YATES: Then in that case you must have read about the murder soon after it happened …

MARIAN: Well?

YATES: Well, you didn't get in touch with me until six days after the murder was committed. (*Slowly*) I should want to know why you waited six days, Miss Hastings.

JEFFREYS enters. He wears his overcoat and carries an envelope.

MARIAN: Oh, I see what you mean. (*A shrug; very sure of herself*) Well you know why. I was abroad and knew nothing about it.

YATES: Yes, of course.

JEFFREYS: Excuse me, sir. This has just arrived. (*He hands YATES the envelope*)

YATES: (*Taking the envelope*) Thank you. (*Smiling at MARIAN*) Miss Hastings is leaving, Sergeant.

JEFFREYS turns and open the door for MARIAN.

YATES: Thank you, Miss Hastings, you've been most helpful.

MARIAN looks at JEFFREYS, then at YATES, finally sweeping out of the office. JEFFREYS closes the door.

JEFFREYS: (*Smiling*) Well, how far did you get?

YATES: How far would you get with a woman like that? (*He tears the page off the pad on the desk*) Ask the Yard to phone the hotel and see if she was there. If they don't get any satisfaction, then we'll get in touch with Passport Control.

JEFFREYS: Right.

YATES opens the envelope, takes out a single sheet of paper, and looks at it.

YATES: They've checked Morris' handwriting with the note that Collins brought us – the one with the bracelet.

JEFFREYS: Well?

YATES: Apparently the handwriting's the same. He wrote it all right.

JEFFREYS: (*Quietly*) I'm not surprised.

YATES: (*Suddenly; putting the note on the desk*) Yes, well, I'm going home for lunch. I've had quite a morning. (*He crosses and picks up his hat and coat*) See you this afternoon.

JEFFREYS: Harry …

YATES: Yes?

JEFFREYS: What about Marian Hastings – was she telling the truth?

YATES: (*Thoughtfully*) I don't think so. I put my money on the Vicar.

JEFFREYS: Then what was she doing in London?

YATES gives JEFFREYS a look.

JEFFREYS: Oh! You think she got a boyfriend and she's playing ducks and drakes with old Goodman?

YATES: The thought had crossed my mind. We'll make a detective out of you yet, Sergeant.

YATES goes out.

CUT TO: The body of a girl on a trailer, which is in a field. The girl appears to be dead and is in almost the same position as FAY COLLINS in Episode One. JOHN HOPEDEAN is sitting at an easel carefully sketching the scene; an artist's reproduction of the FAY COLLINS murder. He continues sketching, looking towards the trailer. Suddenly, we hear the sound of a car drawing to a standstill and HOPEDEAN turns and looks towards the gate which is five or ten yards away. The girl on the trailer hears the noise of the car and sits up, carefully adjusting her skirt and sweater. YATES gets out of his car and walks towards HOPEDEAN.

YATES: Hello, sir! What's going on here?

HOPEDEAN rises. He points to the drawing.

HOPEDEAN: Oh, hello, Inspector! This is for one of the Sunday newspapers …

YATES: (*Looking towards the trailer*) Well, there's no accounting for taste. Isn't that the girl out of the tobacconists?

HOPEDEAN: That's right. Maggie White. She wants to be a model.

YATES looks across at the trailer, where MAGGIE is posing for the INSPECTOR's benefit.

YATES: She's going the right way about it by the look of things.

HOPEDEAN: I suppose there's no news, sir?

90

YATES: No, I'm afraid not. You haven't received
              any more scurrilous letters, I hope, sir?
HOPEDEAN: No, no, thank goodness. Inspector, I saw
              Edward Collins last night.
YATES: Oh, yes, sir?
HOPEDEAN: My wife and I went over to The Bear at
              Belton. He was in the bar. I'm afraid he's
              drinking pretty heavily.
YATES: Yes, I know.
HOPEDEAN: He was shooting his mouth off too, I'm
              afraid.
YATES: Was he, sir – what about?
HOPEDEAN: About you, Inspector. Said you weren't
              doing anything about the murder – just
              sitting on your backside all day. He's in a
              pretty bad way. It's a pity something can't
              be done about it, you know; he's a decent
              chap really. Wish I could help him in some
              way or other.
YATES: (*Quietly*) Yes.

YATES points to HOPEDEAN's drawing.

YATES: Never mind, sir – this'll cheer him up.

*YATES turns and walks back towards his car.
HOPEDEAN stares after him; not sure how to take the
remark.*

CUT TO: The Drawing Room of CLIFTON MORRIS'
Flat. Afternoon.

*CLIFTON MORRIS has his cigarette lighter in his hand.
He is offering a light to DIANA WINSTON. DIANA is
about twenty-eight, an attractive, outspoken, faintly tough
Fleet Street journalist. She is sitting on the settee and
MORRIS is on the arm of a chair, leaning forward towards*

91

her. He wears a lounge suit with a carnation in the lapel of his jacket.

MORRIS: (*Smiling*) I expect you're wondering what this is all about, Miss Winston?

DIANA: Well, I was a little surprised when Mr Thackeray telephoned, I must confess. I was even more surprised when he Shanghaid me into a cab and brought me here.

MORRIS: Why?

DIANA: Your Editor doesn't like me, Mr Morris. He likes my work even less.

MORRIS: Really? I thought he had a very high opinion of you.

DIANA: Well, if he has, he certainly conceals it.

MORRIS: Yes. Well, I don't always agree with Norman, especially about freelance contributors. I read an article of yours some time ago – on the Riviera; Monte Carlo – it was very good.

DIANA: Thank you. (*Smiling*) I wish I'd written it.

MORRIS: Oh. Then – what am I thinking of?

DIANA: (*Amused*) You tell me, Mr Morris.

MORRIS: (*Suddenly remembering*) San Remo! I beg your pardon – San Remo. You did an article on the Italian Riviera.

DIANA: That's right.

MORRIS: About four years ago.

DIANA: … Yes …

MORRIS: It was excellent. First class …

DIANA: I'm surprised you remember it.

MORRIS: Oh, I remember it very well. We did toy with the idea of asking you to write a series for us, but … (*A shrug*) Someone – I forget who it was – didn't think it was a very good idea. However, I didn't get you here just to talk

92

about writing some material for us. I've got another proposition for you – a much more interesting one – at least I think so.

DIANA: (*Looking at him; curious*) Go on, Mr Morris …

MORRIS: (*Not too sure of himself*) Well, first of all … (*With a little laugh*) First of all, I didn't ask you to have a drink, did I?

DIANA: No.

MORRIS: Would you like one?

DIANA: Yes.

MORRIS rises and crosses to the drinks table.

MORRIS: What would you like?

DIANA: Scotch.

MORRIS: (*At the table, turning*) With soda?

DIANA: No – just Scotch.

MORRIS: Oh … (*He pours the drink and brings it across to DIANA*)

DIANA: (*Taking the glass*) Aren't you having one?

MORRIS: Er – yes, I'll have a gin and tonic.

MORRIS returns to the table and mixes himself a drink; his back to DIANA. She looks round the room, taking stock of her surroundings. She gives a little shrug, as if to say to herself – "What can I lose"? MORRIS turns, looks at DIANA and smiles.

MORRIS: Skoal!

DIANA raises her glass and drinks. MORRIS moves towards her.

MORRIS: Now tell me about yourself. What have you been doing during the past eighteen months?

DIANA: I was in Paris for a time, working on a magazine.

MORRIS: Why did you leave?

DIANA: I had a difference of opinion with the Editor.

MORRIS: That can easily happen.

DIANA: Especially in Paris.

MORRIS: (*Smiling*) And since you left Paris?

DIANA: I've been in London doing freelance work.

MORRIS: All the time?

DIANA: Yes, since Christmas.

MORRIS: (*After a moment, pleasantly*) Miss Winston, you'll probably think this is a very extraordinary question, but can you remember where you were – what you were doing exactly – on the night of January 7th?

DIANA: (*Puzzled*) January the 7th?

MORRIS: Yes.

DIANA turns, picks up her bag from the settee, and takes out a small diary.

DIANA: (*Consulting the diary*) That was a Wednesday …

MORRIS: Yes; that's right.

DIANA: (*Looking at the diary again*) I had my hair done in the afternoon. I'm not sure what I did in the evening. I probably worked.

MORRIS: I see.

DIANA looks at him.

DIANA: (*Curious, a shade puzzled*) It is an extraordinary question.

MORRIS: Miss Winston, I'm in a very difficult position. I want you to do me a favour, and I also have a proposition which I want to put to you. I'm not quite sure which to broach first.

DIANA: Is one dependent on the other?

MORRIS: No.

DIANA: (*Surprised*) Are you sure about that, Mr Morris?

MORRIS: I'm quite sure.

DIANA: (*Laughing*) Then it must be a very unique proposition.

MORRIS: I'm thinking of starting a new magazine – a fashion magazine. The Romano people in Italy want to come in with me on the project, the idea being that we publish simultaneously in London and Rome.

DIANA: It sounds exciting.

MORRIS: Well, it could be exciting, and it could be pretty dicey. Now I'll tell you what I'd like you to do. I'd like you to go to Rome for six months; ostensibly for the purpose of writing some articles for us. In actual fact I want you to get to know the Romano people; the whole set-up. At the end of the six months I want a confidential report on them.

DIANA: But what makes you think I can do this?

MORRIS: Can't you?

DIANA: Yes. Yes, I think I can. I get on well with most people – Mr Thackeray excepted – I speak Italian, and I'm pretty good at – well – snooping around.

MORRIS: Let's call it research. All right, that's settled. Three hundred a month, and expenses. (*Smiling*) Now for the second item on the agenda, Miss Winston. On the night of January 7th, a girl called Fay Collins was murdered in a place called Littleshaw. For some obscure reason the police think I had something to do with the murder. (*Shaking his head*) I didn't. I didn't even know Miss Collins. On the night in question, I went to a cinema – the one in Curzon Street. Unfortunately, I went alone.

DIANA: Well?

MORRIS: I've told the police that someone saw me coming out of the cinema. I don't know whether they believe me or not, but – well – obviously the story would be very much stronger if it was corroborated.

DIANA: And you wish me to corroborate it?

MORRIS: (*Quietly; watching her*) Yes.

DIANA: You wish me to tell the police that I saw you coming out of the cinema.

MORRIS: Yes.

DIANA: (*After a pause*) That's all?

MORRIS: Yes – that's all.

DIANA: (*Another pause*) And supposing I don't corroborate your story?

MORRIS: What do you mean?

DIANA: This Italian business …

MORRIS: (*Apparently quite sincere*) The two things are quite separate; I've already told you that.

There is a pause. DIANA continues to look at him.

DIANA: (*Quietly*) Did you go to the cinema?

MORRIS: Yes.

DIANA: What was the film?

MORRIS: "The Cranes are Flying".

DIANA: Did you enjoy it?

MORRIS: Yes. Yes, I did.

DIANA raises her glass, drinks, continues looking at him.

DIANA: (*After a pause, having reached a decision*) So did I, Mr Morris – enormously.

MORRIS: (*Relieved; quietly*) Thank you. (*He turns and puts down his glass*) Now we'll discuss this other business. There are quite a few details. I suggest you drop in the office tomorrow morning or … (*Looks at DIANA*) Or perhaps

96

you'd like to have dinner with me on Friday
night – whichever you prefer?

DIANA: *Pranzianno assienel*, Signor Morris.

MORRIS: What does that mean?

DIANA: (*With a little laugh*) Well, it doesn't mean I'll
drop in the office, Mr Morris.

CUT TO: YATES' Office at Littleshaw Police Station.
Afternoon.

*The telephone on the desk is ringing. JEFFREYS, who is
standing by the desk, wearing his hat and coat, answers it.*

JEFFREYS: (*On the phone*) Hello? Littleshaw 189 …

MORRIS: (*On the other end*) Can I speak to
Inspector Yates, please?

JEFFREYS: I'm sorry, he's out at the moment. Who is
that?

MORRIS: My name is Morris – Clifton Morris.

JEFFREYS: This is Sergeant Jeffreys. Can I take a
message?

CUT TO: The Drawing Room of CLIFTON MORRIS'
Flat. Afternoon.

*DIANA has left, and MORRIS is on the telephone, talking
to JEFFREYS.*

MORRIS: (*On the phone*) Yes. Would you be kind
enough to tell the Inspector I've been in
touch with Miss Winston, and she's
expecting to hear from him. Her address is
14, Rylands Close, Chelsea.

JEFFREYS: (*On the other end of the phone*) 14, Rylands
Close … Yes, all right, sir, I'll tell him that.

MORRIS replaces the receiver; he looks pleased with himself as he crosses towards the bedroom. As he reaches the bedroom door the front doorbell rings, and he turns and goes out into the hall.

CUT TO: The Hall of CLIFTON MORRIS' Flat.

MORRIS opens the front door. A TELEGRAPH BOY stands in the doorway with a telegram in his hand.
BOY: Mr Morris?
MORRIS: Yes.
BOY: (*Handing MORRIS the telegram*) Thank you.
MORRIS closes the door and turns into the hall. He opens the telegram and reads it. It reads: "Expect you tonight sweetie, Kim."

CUT TO: A flashing neon sign advertising The Take-Off Club. The sign shows a typical showgirl, waving a very large Prince of Wales fan.

CUT TO: A Corridor in The Take-Off Club with dressing rooms on either side.

Several showgirls can be seen passing to and fro. HECTOR appears with CLIFTON MORRIS. He opens a dressing room door and enters the room, followed by MORRIS.

CUT TO: KIM STEVENS' Dressing Room at The Take-Off Club. Night.

An irritated and bad-tempered KIM is sitting at the make-up table. She turns as HECTOR enters with CLIFTON MORRIS.

98

HECTOR: You've got a visitor.

KIM: I can see that.

HECTOR: (*Smugly*) And Monty says he's changing the running order tomorrow.

KIM: You can tell Monty to take a powder.

KIM crosses and gently pushes HECTOR into the corridor.

KIM: And while you're at it, tell that baby-faced band leader to keep his eyes on the music …

HECTOR: (*As the door closes on him*) Are you referring to Bruce?

KIM: (*Irritated, turning away from the door*) He's a dead-beat; he really is … Were you out in front tonight?

MORRIS: No.

KIM: Congratulations! My God, what an audience! Next week, the Zoo. (*Moving towards the chest of drawers*) Sit down – I'll get you a drink.

MORRIS: Miss Stevens, I haven't a lot of time so …

KIM: (*Turning*) Have you still got ants in your pants? What am I – the plague? (*She starts to mix a drink*)

MORRIS: (*Watching KIM*) I got your telegram …

KIM: Sure, I know that. You wouldn't be here if you hadn't got it, sweetie. (*Moving towards MORRIS with the drink*) Here …

MORRIS: (*Shaking his head*) No thank you.

KIM: Don't you drink?

MORRIS: Yes, I drink.

KIM: But you're pretty choosey who you drink with – is that it?

MORRIS: That's it – exactly.

KIM looks at MORRIS, annoyed; then she raises the glass and drinks herself.

KIM: Okay, Mr Tycoon. I've got a proposition for you. I've spoken to my friend.

MORRIS: Your friend?

KIM: The gentleman with the letter.

MORRIS: I thought you had the letter?

KIM: (*Shaking her head*) No, I said I could get it for you. You said – how much? Remember?

MORRIS: Yes, I remember.

KIM turns towards the dressing table.

KIM: (*A shade embarrassed*) Well, it'll cost you eighteen thousand pounds.

MORRIS looks at her in amazement, and then starts to laugh. After a moment he sits on the arm of the chair.

MORRIS: Did you say eighteen thousand pounds?

KIM: (*Arranging her hair at the mirror*) That's what I said.

MORRIS: Do you think I'm crazy?

KIM: (*Turning and looking at MORRIS*) You wrote that letter, didn't you?

MORRIS: Yes.

KIM: (*Nodding*) Then you're crazy. (*She turns and looks in the mirror again*)

A pause.

MORRIS: How do I know your friend's got the letter?

KIM opens a drawer and takes out a sheet of paper.

MORRIS: Just because you've got a recording of a telephone conversation, it doesn't mean to say …

KIM interrupts him by handing over the sheet of paper.

KIM: With my friend's compliments – it's a photocopy.

MORRIS looks at the photocopy.

MORRIS: (*After a pause*) All right, he's got the letter and he wants eighteen thousand pounds for it. What

	happens if he doesn't get the eighteen thousand?
KIM:	You know what'll happen – he sends it to the police.
MORRIS:	And I shall swear I didn't write it.
KIM:	You can swear until you're blue in the face, Duckie. It's your handwriting. That letter proves you knew Fay Collins – it proves you wanted to see her.
MORRIS:	Yes, but I didn't see her …
KIM:	Oh, yes you did! You made the appointment on the phone.
MORRIS:	But I didn't keep it.

KIM looks at MORRIS, a shade surprised.

KIM:	(*Quietly*) I think you did.
MORRIS:	(*Smiling*) But I can prove I didn't. (*He rises*) I'm sorry to disappoint your friend, but I have an alibi. I went to the cinema the night the murder was committed – fortunately someone saw me there.
KIM:	I don't believe you!
MORRIS:	It's true.
KIM:	Well, even if it is true – even if you have an alibi – that letter's still important.
MORRIS:	I agree. But not so important as it was. (*Smiling shaking his head*) I'm certainly not paying eighteen thousand pounds for it.
KIM:	Good Heavens, sweetie, you're a wealthy man, what's eighteen thousand …
MORRIS:	(*Interrupting her*) Yes, and do you know why I'm a wealthy man, Miss Stevens?
KIM:	No, tell me, Buster. Give me the first easy lesson.

MORRIS: (*Quietly*) Because people like you, and your boyfriend, underrate me. (*Not raising his voice; yet with authority*) Tell him my price is eight hundred pounds – for the tape and the letter.

KIM: (*Surprised*) Eight hundred quid!

MORRIS: That's right.

KIM: You're up the wall! Do you think he'll accept that?

MORRIS: (*Picking up his hat*) Let me know. (*He moves towards the door*) Send me another telegram … sweetie …

CLIFTON MORRIS opens the door and goes out into the corridor.

CUT TO: Outside a block of flats in Mayfair.

A taxi draws to a standstill outside the entrance. CLIFTON MORRIS gets out of the cab, pays the driver and goes into the building. He is returning home from his meeting with KIM.

CUT TO: The Drawing Room of CLIFTON MORRIS' Flat. Night.

MORRIS enters the room from the hall, suddenly stopping dead in his tracks. The body of DIANA WINSTON is on the floor near the settee; she is dead – strangled. A heavily built man – CHIEF SUPERINTENDENT NASH – is kneeling down by the body talking to the police surgeon, DR COUSINS. A uniformed police sergeant stands on the other side of the body.

COUSINS: (*To NASH*) Oh, definitely strangled, sir – and I should say she's been dead about an hour.

At the head of the small group and facing the hall stands HARRY YATES. He is holding MORRIS' evening dress scarf. He looks up, his eyes on CLIFTON MORRIS, his expression serious – the scarf dangling from his hand.

END OF EPISODE THREE

EPISODE FOUR

OPEN TO: The Drawing Room of CLIFTON MORRIS'
Flat. Night.

SUPERINTENDENT NASH rises from his examination of
DIANA WINSTON's body and looks across the room
towards the hall and CLIFTON MORRIS.

MORRIS slowly advances towards the group.

MORRIS: (*Stunned*) What's happened?

NASH: Mr Morris?

MORRIS: Yes …

NASH: (*With authority*) Do you know this woman?

MORRIS: (*Looking down at the body, dazed*) Yes, I
             do … Her name's Diana Winston … (*To*
             YATES) what is it? For God's sake tell me
             – what's happened?

YATES: (*Nodding towards NASH*) Superintendent
             Nash received an anonymous phone call
             saying that a girl had been murdered at
             this address.

NASH: (*Looking at MORRIS*) The door was on the
             latch. We found Miss Winston …

MORRIS: Is – is she dead?

COUSINS: (*Nodding*) Yes – she's been strangled.

YATES: (*Holding up the scarf*) With your scarf,
             Mr Morris.

CUT TO: A small outer office – used as a filing room –
at New Scotland Yard. Night.

SERGEANT DALY, a faintly disgruntled man in his early
forties, sits at his desk and proceeds to check the contents
of a small index file, making notes on a sheet of paper as
he does so. DETECTIVE SERGEANT JEFFREYS enters.
He wears a trench coat and carries his hat.

JEFFREYS: Good evening. I understand Inspector
               Yates is here …
DALY: Who are you?
JEFFREYS: Jeffreys. Hertfordshire C.I.D.
DALY: (*Nodding towards the door which leads to
               the   main   office*) He's   with   the
               Superintendent. I can't disturb him.
JEFFREYS: I'm afraid you'll have to. (*He takes a
               notebook out of his pocket*) Lend me a
               pencil, Sergeant.

DALY looks at him; hesitant, then hands over a pencil.

JEFFREYS: You're working late.
DALY: Late? Don't be silly, this is my day off!
               You plain clothes men don't know you're
               born.

*JEFFREYS grins; then thoughtfully starts to write in the
notebook.*

CUT TO: The Office of CHIEF SUPERINTENDENT
NASH. Night.
This is a large, pleasant room facing a courtyard.

*NASH is sitting behind his desk. YATES on the left of him.
MORRIS sits facing NASH with a uniformed police clerk
on his right. The clerk is discreetly taking shorthand notes
and remains in the background.*

NASH: You say the scarf was in a drawer in the
               dressing room?
MORRIS: Yes; I only wear it with a dinner jacket.
               Although oddly enough I very nearly put it
               on this afternoon. I wish to Heaven I had
               now.
NASH: What time was it when you left the flat?
MORRIS: About half past five.

NASH: That was after your interview with Miss Winston?

MORRIS: That's right.

NASH: *(Looking at the pad on his desk)* So after your talk to Miss Winston you went to the office; you stayed there until about half past seven; you then had dinner at your Club, and went back to the office again at about a quarter to nine?

MORRIS: Yes.

YATES: And stayed there until – when?

MORRIS: Until about … *(He looks at his watch)* … an hour ago.

YATES: Was there anybody else at the office? Your secretary?

MORRIS: No; that was one of the reasons why I went back there. I had some work to do, and I wanted to be alone.

NASH: So in actual fact no one saw you?

MORRIS: *(Irritated)* No one saw me at the office, but plenty of people saw me at the Club.

NASH: Yes, but that was earlier in the evening. We're interested in your movements from about half past nine.

MORRIS: From half past nine, until the time I arrived at the flat, I was sitting in a very large office, at a very large desk, studying a very large expense account.

YATES: *(Smiling)* Mr Morris, I understand you telephoned me this afternoon?

MORRIS: Yes, I did. I tried to get in touch with you about Miss Winston. She remembered seeing me at the cinema the night Fay Collins was murdered.

109

YATES: (*Quietly*) I see.

MORRIS: I only hope to heaven you do see,
              Inspector, because now she's dead you've
              only got my word for it.

YATES: That thought had occurred to me.

The door opens and DALY enters.

DALY: (*To NASH*) Excuse me, sir.

NASH: Yes – what is it?

DALY: (*To YATES*) There's a Sergeant Jeffreys
              here – he asked me to give you this,
              Inspector.

DALY hands the note to YATES.

YATES: Thank you.

*YATES reads the note: smiles, then hands it to NASH who
looks at it, puts it down on the desk and rises.*

NASH: (*Abruptly*) All right, Mr Morris. Thank
              you very much. If we want to get in touch
              with you, we know where you are.

*MORRIS looks at NASH, obviously surprised by this
abrupt dismissal. DALY crosses and opens the door,
MORRIS hesitates, then nods to YATES and goes out.*

NASH: (*To DALY*) Tell Jeffreys to come in.

DALY: Yes, sir.

DALY goes out. NASH picks up the note from the desk.

NASH: Why the devil didn't he tell us he'd been
              to "Take-Off".

YATES: (*Quietly*) It's a good question, sir.

*NASH looks across at YATES, then turns towards the door
as JEFFREYS enters.*

NASH: (*To JEFFREYS*) What time did he leave
              the Club?

JEFFREYS: About half past eight, sir …

NASH: And he stayed at the office until –?

110

JEFFREYS: Until about ten o'clock, and then he took a cab to the "Take-Off". He left there about a quarter to eleven.

NASH: You're sure he didn't leave the office before ten?

JEFFREYS: I'm positive, sir.

NASH: Where is the office?

JEFFREYS: It's in South Audley Street, just off Park Lane.

NASH: A modern block?

JEFFREYS: Yes.

NASH: How many entrances?

JEFFREYS: Two; but I had a man on each, sir.

NASH nods apparently satisfied.

NASH: Thank you, Sergeant.

JEFFREYS smiles, nods to YATES and returns to the outer office.

CUT TO: The Drawing Room of Greensteps. The Following Morning.

EDWARD COLLINS is sitting in an armchair facing HARRY YATES. He has been drinking heavily: he is in a bad mood, irritable and angry. He has a glass of whisky in his hand and there is an open newspaper on his lap.

EDWARD: … It's absolutely ridiculous! Just sheer blazing incompetence! (*Rising*) How much proof do you want before you arrest this chap? (*Flourishing the newspaper*) He's already murdered two people …

YATES: That's just your opinion, sir.

EDWARD: What do you mean – just my opinion? It sticks out a mile. I suppose the fact that he's a millionaire though …

111

YATES:	(*Interrupting*) Look, Mr Collins, I came here because you said you had something to tell me …
EDWARD:	I have something to tell you! (*He drinks*) I'm dissatisfied – extremely dissatisfied with the way you're handling this case.
YATES:	I'll bear that in mind.
EDWARD:	Never mind bearing it in mind! Get weaving … Get a move on … Arrest the swine.
YATES:	(*Unperturbed*) And what would you suggest we charge him with, sir?
EDWARD:	You know damn well what to charge him with! … He murdered my sister …
YATES:	(*Quietly*) How do you know that, sir?
EDWARD:	How do I know it? The whole world knows it! Everybody knows it! Everybody except the police … (*He moves towards YATES, pointing at him*) Marian Hastings saw Morris … She saw him here, in Littleshaw, the night Fay was murdered …
YATES:	And what does that prove?
EDWARD:	For Heaven's sake, haven't you got any imagination? Have you got to have everything stuck right under your ruddy noses? I'll tell you what it proves!
YATES:	Yes, sir?
EDWARD:	It proves Clifton Morris knew my sister; it proves he had a date with Fay the night she was murdered.
YATES:	(*Quietly*) Go on, sir …
EDWARD:	What do you mean, 'go on' …?
YATES:	Go on. I'm interested …

112

EDWARD: (*With a derisive laugh*) Ah! He's interested ... Well, that's something, I suppose ... Three weeks after the murder, Inspector Harry Yates is still interested ... (*He moves nearer to YATES: bitterly*) Well, just how interested are you, Inspector? Are you interested in me, my feelings, what I've been through during the past three weeks? Would you like to know what's been going on in this little head of mine?

YATES: (*Quietly*) Yes, I would. I would, indeed, sir.

EDWARD: Well, I'll tell you! I've been thinking about you. I've been thinking what a hopeless, inefficient person you are.

YATES: (*Pleasantly*) Have you, sir?

EDWARD: Yes, I have. Hopeless; inefficient.

YATES: (*With the suggestion of a smile*) Well, you've got that off your chest, Mr Collins. I hope you feel better.

EDWARD: Now don't get patronising. For Heaven's sake don't you get patronising!

YATES: I think perhaps you've had too much to drink, sir. If you do happen to remember why you sent for me – let me know. I shall be delighted to call again.

YATES picks up his hat from the settee and goes out into the hall. EDWARD stands looking towards the hall, then as we hear the front door close, he turns towards the drinks table. He puts his glass down on the table, hesitates a moment, and then crosses to the telephone. He stands by the telephone, undecided, then he picks up the receiver and dials a number. There is a pause. We hear the number ringing out.

113

PBX OPERATOR: (*On the other end of the line*)
                Mayfair 1874 … New World Publications
                …
EDWARD: Can I speak to Mr Clifton Morris?
OPERATOR: Who is that calling?
EDWARD: (*Aggressively*) Tell him my name is
            Edward Collins and I want to talk to him!
OPERATOR: One moment, Mr Collins.

CUT TO: *YATES is walking down a country road after his interview with EDWARD COLLINS. A small car – driven by the REVEREND NIGEL MATTHEWS – appears and slowly draws to a standstill.*

MATTHEWS: (*Pleasantly surprised*) Inspector!
YATES: Oh, hello, there!
MATTHEWS: Can I give you a lift?
YATES: Why, yes – thank you, Padre.

YATES gets into the passenger seat by the side of MATTHEWS.

The PADRE changes gear and the car continues down the road.

CUT TO: *MATTHEWS and YATES sitting side by side in the car. MATTHEWS is driving.*

YATES: This is a lucky coincidence, Mr Matthews.
            I wanted to have a chat with you.
MATTHEWS: Oh, splendid! Are you on your way to the
          station?
YATES: No; I'm going home. Drop me on the
            corner of Layton Avenue.
MATTHEWS: Delighted.
YATES: I've just been paying Mr Collins a visit.
MATTHEWS: (*Significantly*) And how did you find
          Edward?

114

YATES: (*Smiling*) Aggressive.

MATTHEWS: Yes, I'm not surprised. I think he's aggressive with most people these days. I know I've had one or two very unpleasant interviews with him. He's been drinking rather heavily, you know.

YATES: He still is.

MATTHEWS: (*With a nod*) T't. T't. I thought so. It's an awful pity. He's such a nice person when you get to know him.

YATES: I'll take your word for it, Padre.

MATTHEWS: (*Nodding*) I know. I know, my dear fellow. I know exactly how you feel. (*A slight pause*) Did you say you wanted to talk to me about something?

YATES: Oh, yes. (*Hesitantly*) Have you seen the papers this morning?

MATTHEWS: No, I'm afraid I haven't. I've been frightfully busy. My housekeeper's away and I find that if I once start to read the morning … (*Stops: curious*) But why do you ask if I've seen the papers?

YATES: A girl called Diana Winston was found strangled last night in Clifton Morris's flat. Unfortunately for Morris she's the girl who saw him at the cinema the night Fay Collins was murdered.

MATTHEWS: But this is dreadful news – really dreadful …

YATES: Yes, it was quite a shock to Mr Morris, I'm afraid.

MATTHEWS: But what was the girl doing in the flat? Had Terry invited her there?

YATES: No; apparently not. Padre, when I was talking to you the other day about Clifton Morris, I mentioned this girl to you.

MATTHEWS: Yes, you did. I remember now.

YATES: Did you, by any chance, mention her name to anyone?

MATTHEWS: Why no, of course not! Why on earth … Oh, dear! Oh dear, I've just remembered …

YATES: (*Looking at him: quietly*) What have you remembered, sir?

MATTHEWS: (*Embarrassed*) Well, after we had our little chat I bumped into Mr Goodman.

YATES: Go on, Padre.

MATTHEWS: He started talking about Fay Collins and Clifton Morris – Terry.

YATES: Well?

MATTHEWS: Well, I'm afraid I rather lost my temper with him. You see, he seemed to take it for granted that Terry had committed the murder – just wouldn't listen to any other point of view.

YATES: I see.

MATTHEWS: Naturally, I defended Terry. I felt I had to. But I'm afraid in doing so I inadvertently mentioned Miss Winston.

YATES: (*Pleasantly*) Oh, well, that's all right, sir. Don't worry.

MATTHEWS: I'm awfully sorry, Inspector. I didn't really intend to betray a confidence.

YATES: (*Interrupting him*) I should have done exactly the same under the circumstances, sir.

A pause.

116

YATES: Mr Matthews, you remember what you told me   about Miss Hastings – about seeing her in   London?

MATTHEWS: Yes.

YATES: Well, I spoke to Miss Hastings about it – without mentioning your name, of course. She ridiculed the whole idea. She swore that on January the 9th she was in Chamonix. She actually gave me the name of the hotel she was staying at.

MATTHEWS: And did you write to the hotel?

YATES: We did better than that – we telephoned them. Miss Hastings was in Chamonix, sir. She arrived there on January 9th.

MATTHEWS: (*Quietly*) I see.

YATES: So you couldn't possibly have seen her in Regent Street.

A pause. MATTHEWS turns and looks at YATES.

MATTHEWS: (*Quite simply: with almost a suggestion of a smile*) But I did, Inspector.

CUT TO: *A man is sitting in the driving seat of a car (a shooting break) outside of YATES' cottage. He is reading a newspaper. After a moment he lowers the newspaper, and we recognise ALISTAIR GOODMAN. Through the windscreen of the car, we can see YATES at the end of the evening, getting out of MATTHEWS' car and saying goodbye to the PADRE. GOODMAN obviously recognises YATES: he gets out of the shooting brake, still holding the newspaper.*

CUT TO: *YATES joining GOODMAN at the side of the shooting brake.*

YATES: Hello, Mr Goodman! What are you doing here?

GOODMAN: I'm waiting for my fiancée. Twenty minutes ago, she was only going to be five minutes.

YATES: Where is she – with my wife?

GOODMAN: Yes. Mrs Yates has bought a new dress; she's trying it on.

YATES: You mean she'd tried it on, and I've bought it! Come along inside and I'll give you a drink …

GOODMAN: No, thanks. (*He looks at his watch*) We're supposed to be at Amersham by half past one. Put a bomb under the pair of them, Inspector!

YATES: I'll try. (*Turning; then noticing the newspaper in GOODMAN's hand*) I suppose you've been reading about this murder case?

GOODMAN: Yes, I have. What an extraordinary business. It's the same chap, of course, isn't it?

YATES: The same chap?

GOODMAN: Yes – the fellow that Marian saw with Fay Collins – What's his name? (*He looks at the newspaper*) Ah, yes … here we are … Clifton Morris …

YATES: Oh, I see what you mean.

GOODMAN: Don't think I'm rude, old man. But how many people has this character got to bump off before you boys really get the bit between your teeth?

118

YATES: Oh, we're not fussy, sir.

GOODMAN: You're certainly not. Anyway, it's perfectly obvious he did this one. Even you chaps must realise that.

YATES: Really, sir?

GOODMAN: Why, dammit, man, yes! Don't be silly – she was found in his flat. (*He looks at the newspaper again*) A jolly good looker, too – poor kid.

YATES: Yes. (*Casually*) Did you know her, Mr Goodman?

GOODMAN looks up from the newspaper; very surprised.

GOODMAN: Know her? What – me?

YATES: Yes.

GOODMAN: Good heavens, no! Whatever gave you that idea?

YATES: I wondered, sir – that's all.

GOODMAN: Well, you must have had a reason for asking a question like that?

YATES: I just thought perhaps you might have met her, sir – that's all.

GOODMAN: Yes, but why? Why should you think that?

YATES: She came down to Littleshaw.

GOODMAN: When?

YATES: I don't know when exactly. (*He looks at GOODMAN for a moment*) But she bought a dress from your fiancée. (*Suddenly smiling; then turning towards the gate*) I'll see what I can do about that bomb.

GOODMAN watches YATES as he walks through the garden towards the cottage.

119

CUT TO: The Living Room of YATES' Cottage. Day.

JILL and MARIAN HASTINGS are discussing clothes as YATES enters the room from the hall. JILL is sitting on the arm of the settee with MARIAN facing her in an armchair. JILL wears a new dress and there is an open cardboard box on the settee. MARIAN has a cocktail glass in her hand and wears a fur stole.

MARIAN: … My dear Mrs Yates, you'd be surprised what some people will wear. I get dumpy little women coming into my shop who are convinced – but positively convinced – that they look like Barbara Goalen. And when I eventually summon up enough courage to tell them that the new line wasn't exactly inspired by a 44 hip, they go out of their way to …

MARIAN breaks off as YATES enters.

YATES: (*Coming into the room*) Good morning, Miss Hastings.

MARIAN: (*Putting down the cocktail glass*) Oh, hello, Inspector!

YATES: (*Crossing and kissing his wife*) Hello, darling. (*To MARIAN*) I've just been talking to a furious looking man in a shooting brake. Does he belong to you?

MARIAN: Ye gods, Alistair! I'd forgotten all about the poor darling. (*Looks at her watch*) We're supposed to be in Amersham at half past one.

JILL: (*Showing YATES her dress*) This is the dress I was telling you about, Harry. Do you like it?

YATES: (*Hardly looking at her*) Yes, I do. How much was it?

JILL: How much was – (*To MARIAN*) Isn't it extraordinary! It doesn't matter what I buy …

YATES: (*Stopping her: turning towards MARIAN*) Just a minute, Jill! Miss Hastings, I know you're in a hurry at the moment, but I would like to have a word with you. I dropped in the shop this morning, but you'd just left.

MARIAN: (*Puzzled*) Yes, of course. What is it, Inspector?

YATES: There was another murder last night – a girl called Diana Winston.

MARIAN: Yes, Alistair was telling me about it. Apparently, she was a friend of Clifton Morris's.

YATES: (*Nodding*) I saw the poor girl soon after it happened. She was wearing a blue dress. It was bought from your shop, Miss Hastings.

MARIAN: (*Moving towards YATES: surprised*) Are you sure?

YATES: It has a tab inside the collar with your name on it.

The front doorbell starts ringing.

MARIAN: What did you say her name was – Diana Winston?

YATES: Yes.

MARIAN: I don't remember anyone of that name – She's certainly not one of my regular customers.

JILL: (*Going out into the hall*) That's probably Mr Goodman.

MARIAN: Yes … (*She hesitates; then turns towards YATES again*) What did she look like, this girl?

121

YATES: She was about twenty-eight – blonde – about five foot seven; quite good looking. There's a picture of her in the Daily Echo.

MARIAN: (*Suddenly remembering*) Oh, yes, of course there is! I've seen it. (*Thoughtfully; shaking her head*) I'm sorry, Inspector, I'm afraid I didn't recognise her.

YATES: Well, perhaps if you go through your accounts it might help to jog your memory, Miss Hastings.

MARIAN: Yes, it might. I'll do that.

JILL returns with JOHN HOPEDEAN. He wears an overcoat and is carrying a morning newspaper. He looks a little tense, and a shade worried.

JILL: Harry, Mr Hopedean would like to have a word with you.

YATES: Oh, come in, sir!

HOPEDEAN: (*Looking at MARIAN*) I'm sorry if I'm disturbing you.

YATES: No – no, that's all right. You know Miss Hastings, of course?

HOPEDEAN: Yes, of course. (*To MARIAN*) Hello, Marian …

MARIAN: (*A shade off-hand*) Hello, John – how are you?

HOPEDEAN: I'm – quite well, thank you. (*With a nod towards the hall*) Your fiancé seems to be in a rather bad mood. Wouldn't even say good afternoon.

MARIAN: Oh, lord, that means he's beginning to sulk! I must fly before the dry rot sets in!

MARIAN goes out into the hall followed by JILL.

YATES:	(*To HOPEDEAN*) What is it you wanted to see me about, sir? Have you received another poison pen letter?
HOPEDEAN:	What? Oh, no, no thank goodness, I haven't had any more of those wretched things. (*Displaying the newspaper*) It's about this murder case, Inspector. I was absolutely bowled over when I read about it.
YATES:	Were you, sir?
HOPEDEAN:	Why, yes! Don't you realise this is the second friend of mine that's been murdered?
YATES:	(*Apparently surprised*) Was Diana Winston a friend of yours, then?
HOPEDEAN:	Yes. Not a very intimate friend, mark you – not like – well – like Fay Collins, for instance. But nevertheless, she was a friend of mine.
YATES:	I see. Yes, I can see why you were bowled over, Mr Hopedean. When did you last see Miss Winston?
HOPEDEAN:	Oh, I haven't seen her for ages. Not for eighteen months. I thought she was in Paris.
YATES:	She did work in Paris for a time, I understand.
HOPEDEAN:	Yes, she was with the Flaubert people. I thought she was still with them, as a matter of fact.
YATES:	When did you first meet Miss Winston?
HOPEDEAN:	About three years ago. I illustrated some articles she'd written for a magazine; there was even some talk of us doing a book

123

together. We used to see quite a bit of each other, in the days – but nothing came of it. (*Quickly; embarrassed*) The book, I mean.

YATES: Where did you used to meet – in London?

HOPEDEAN: Yes.

YATES: At her flat?

HOPEDEAN: No; I've been to her flat, of course, but usually we used to meet in bars and restaurants – those sort of places.

YATES: I see. Did she ever come down to Littleshaw?

HOPEDEAN: Not to my knowledge.

YATES: You never invited her down here?

HOPEDEAN: Good Lord, no! I wasn't such a fool as to do that!

YATES: Your wife knows nothing about your association with Miss Winston, I take it?

HOPEDEAN: No, she doesn't. That's why I decided to see you, Inspector. I thought if you suddenly discovered I was a friend of hers you might come barging down to the house and, well – ask a lot of very awkward questions.

YATES: (*Pleasantly*) I may still ask a lot of very awkward questions.

HOPEDEAN: Yes, but – not in front of the wife, I hope.

YATES: (*Moving towards the settee*) Mr Hopedean, I appreciate your frankness in coming here, but I should appreciate it even more if you were completely honest with me.

HOPEDEAN: What do you mean?

YATES: Were you having an affair with Miss Winston?

124

HOPEDEAN: Good Lord, no! I've told you, we worked together – we collaborated. You know, it really is quite extraordinary, everybody seems to think I'm having an affair with someone! The whole of Littleshaw, my wife included, are quite convinced I was having an affair with Fay Collins, and now you – which probably means the whole of the local police force – are equally convinced I was having one with Diana. Quite honestly, Inspector, I'm beginning to think I'm a bit of an eccentric. I go to bed to sleep.

YATES laughs and sits on the arm of the settee.

YATES: Tell me: did you know Miss Winston was a friend of Clifton Morris's?

HOPEDEAN: No. Was she a friend of his? This paper says he hardly knew her.

YATES: She was found in his flat.

HOPEDEAN: Yes, I know, but that doesn't necessarily mean he knew her.

YATES: What's the other explanation?

HOPEDEAN: Morris is a very wealthy man. It seems to be the fashion these days to despise wealth. (*A shrug*) Who knows – perhaps someone doesn't like him.

YATES: You mean – he's being framed?

HOPEDEAN: Yes. Hadn't the thought occurred to you, Inspector?

YATES: (*Looking at HOPEDEAN, after a moment*) Only in a vague sort of way, sir.

JILL enters from the hall.

JILL: (*To HOPEDEAN*) Excuse me. (*To YATES*) It's Monday, Harry …

125

JILL goes into the kitchen, closing the door behind her. YATES and HOPEDEAN look towards the kitchen, then at each other. YATES gives a bewildered little shrug and HOPEDEAN laughs.

CUT TO: The Kitchen of YATES's Cottage. Day.
This is a bright, newly-painted, well-stocked kitchen, complete with Frigidaire, cupboards, etc. There is a table, which is set for lunch – cold meat and salad.

JILL gets a butter dish out of one of the cupboards and then sits at the table. She is eating her lunch when YATES enters.

YATES: Jill, what did you mean by … (*It dawns on him*) Oh, we're having lunch in here!

JILL: That's right, darling. We do every Monday – remember?

YATES: Oh, Lord, yes.

YATES opens the Frigidaire and takes out a jug. He pours himself a glass of milk.

JILL: (*Busy with her lunch*) Has Rembrandt departed?

YATES: Yes.

JILL: I don't like that man.

YATES: (*Taking his place at the table*) You don't know him.

JILL: I still don't like him. He should wear a beard. All artists should wear beards.

YATES: Don't be silly, darling, he's not that sort of artist.

A pause.

JILL: Well, what's happened? Has somebody been sending him some more of those horrible letters?

126

YATES: No – at least, he says not.

JILL: (*Looking up*) Well – don't you believe him?

YATES: (*After a moment; quietly*) No.

JILL: (*Surprised*) Why not?

YATES: Because he received one this morning.

JILL: Are you sure?

YATES: (*Quietly; nodding*) I'm positive. (*He looks at her*) I sent it. (*He starts to eat his lunch*)

JILL stares at YATES.

CUT TO: The Drawing Room of Greensteps. Late Afternoon.

CLIFTON MORRIS is standing facing EDWARD who is sitting in the armchair, the walking stick by his side. EDWARD has an empty glass in his hand. MORRIS wears an overcoat; his hat is on the settee. He looks down at EDWARD, obviously annoyed and irritated.

MORRIS: … There's no point in my staying here. You've quite obviously already made up your mind about me.

EDWARD: Have I, Mr Morris?

MORRIS: Yes, and nothing I can say will make you change it, I'm sure of that.

EDWARD: (*Rising; picking up his stick*) Oh, I don't know. I wouldn't be quite so dogmatic if I were you. You have a very persuasive tongue and like our mutual friend Yates I'm open to conviction.

MORRIS: I can only tell you, once again, that I did not murder your sister!

127

EDWARD: And I can only tell you, once again, that I don't believe you.

MORRIS: (*Exasperated*) Why don't you believe me?

EDWARD: Because you're a liar! You've lied about everything; right from the very beginning you've lied! (*Shaking his head*) Why the police haven't arrested you, I just can't imagine.

MORRIS: Perhaps they don't share your opinion of me, Mr Collins.

EDWARD: Oh, yes, they do. They think you did it all right, I'm sure of that.

MORRIS: But how can they possibly think that, when I didn't even know your sister?

EDWARD: (*Turning on MORRIS*) You didn't know her?

MORRIS: (*Hesitantly*) No …

EDWARD: Then why did you come here this afternoon?

MORRIS: Because I wanted to meet you, and – I was curious.

EDWARD: Curious?

MORRIS: Yes; your message said you had something to show me.

EDWARD: Ah, yes … (*Crosses to the drinks table*) … Yes, well in view of what you've just said that no longer applies I'm afraid.

MORRIS: What do you mean?

EDWARD: (*Putting his glass down*) I found a book which I thought might interest you. I was mistaken. (*Turning; looking at MORRIS*) My sister had it – it was in her room upstairs. She must have been reading it the last time she came down here.

128

MORRIS: What is this book?

EDWARD: It's a book of poems.

MORRIS: May I see it?

EDWARD: No …

MORRIS: Why not?

EDWARD: (*Moving towards the drum top table*)
            Because if you were telling me the truth
            just now, and you didn't know Fay, then
            the book can't possibly interest you.

MORRIS: Nevertheless, I'd like to see it.

EDWARD: (*After a pause*) Why?

MORRIS: (*Quietly; yet with authority*) I'd like to see
            it, Mr Collins.

Another pause.

EDWARD: (*Suddenly; with the suggestion of a smile*)
            Very well – you shall.

*EDWARD picks up a small book off the drum top table and
without warning tosses it across to MORRIS who catches
it.*

EDWARD: The first page, Mr Morris, is the
            interesting one.

*MORRIS looks at EDWARD, then slowly opens the book.
On the first page is a book plate – ex-libris – on the page
with the name "CLIFTON MORRIS" written in MORRIS's
handwriting. MORRIS slowly looks up and an expression
of astonishment suddenly registers on his face. EDWARD
has moved forward and is now standing by the telephone
table. He holds a revolver in his hand – it is pointing at
CLIFTON MORRIS.*

EDWARD: (*Tensely*) Do you still say you didn't know
            Fay?

MORRIS: (*Obviously frightened*) Now look, don't let's
            be stupid about this. This book doesn't
            prove anything …

129

EDWARD: (*Raising the revolver*) Doesn't it? It's your book!

MORRIS: Yes, I know that, but surely …

EDWARD: And Fay borrowed it from you. You don't usually borrow books from people you don't know!

MORRIS: (*Still frightened; a shade desperate*) Yes, of course, I realise that! But let me explain … (*Suddenly tense*) Mr Collins, wait …

EDWARD shakes his head and is just about to fire the revolver when the telephone rings. The sound of the bell takes him completely by surprise and without thinking he turns and looks towards the table. MORRIS immediately springs forward and makes a grab for the revolver. EDWARD loses his balance and falls against the drum top table, knocking it to the ground, the telephone falling with the table. MORRIS and EDWARD continue their struggle for the revolver, and from the overturned telephone receiver, can be heard a man's voice (YATES') puzzled and bewildered by the noise in the room. Suddenly, EDWARD slips again and falls across the over-turned table, hitting his head on the corner of the settee. He lies quite still. MORRIS looks down at him; worried and frightened. He kneels down and feels his pulse; for a moment he looks a little concerned, then EDWARD stirs, and with a look of relief, MORRIS rises. He looks round the room, then notices the book on the floor near the table and the revolver. He picks up the book, moves as if to pick up the receiver, and then changes his mind and turns towards the settee again. EDWARD is still unconscious. MORRIS looks at him for a moment, then glances at his watch and hesitates – suddenly he reaches a decision, picks up his hat and goes out into the hall.

CUT TO: *MORRIS comes out of Greensteps and runs across to a stationary Bentley, parked near the main gate. He jumps into the car and after a moment the car drives away.*

CUT TO: The Drawing Room of Greensteps.

JEFFREYS picks up the revolver, looking at YATES and EDWARD COLLINS. EDWARD is now on the settee; dazed and a little confused, but he has recovered consciousness. YATES is sitting by EDWARD, at the foot of the settee, carefully watching him.

YATES: Do you feel any better?

EDWARD: (*Annoyed with himself*) I'm all right.

YATES: You don't look all right. What happened?

EDWARD: (*Irritated*) I – I don't know what happened.

YATES: (*Aggressively*) You don't know?

JEFFREYS crosses and hands YATES the revolver. YATES takes it, looks at EDWARD, who is watching him, then examines the gun. JEFFREYS replaces the telephone on the table, then goes out into the hall.

YATES: (*To EDWARD*) Is this yours?

EDWARD: Yes.

YATES: How long have you had it?

EDWARD: (*Obviously lying*) About – about six months.

YATES: (*Shaking his head*) You bought it just over a week ago from a shop in Camden Town. You paid twelve pounds for it, and you haven't got a licence.

EDWARD looks at YATES.

YATES: Do you think I don't know what's going on around here? Do you think I'm a fool?

EDWARD sits up slightly; he rubs the back of his head.

131

EDWARD: Why did you come? What happened?

YATES: (*Nodding towards the telephone*) I phoned
            you. I heard the racket going on. It didn't
            sound as if you were having fun and
            games.

EDWARD: We weren't.

YATES: Who was it?

EDWARD doesn't answer.

YATES: Well? (*Angrily*) I'm asking you, who it
            was?

EDWARD: Clifton Morris ...

YATES: (*Surprised*) Morris? What was he doing
            here?

*EDWARD rises from the settee, picks up his stick and
crosses to the drinks table.*

EDWARD: (*Turning, as he reaches the table, dazed*)
            What did you say?

YATES: (*Moving towards EDWARD*) Why did you
            send for Clifton Morris?

EDWARD: I wanted to take a good look at the swine.

YATES: (*Holding the revolver*) Did you threaten
            him with this?

EDWARD: (*Tensely; still angry with himself*) Yes ...

YATES: You idiot! Surely to God you didn't think
            you could get away with that sort of thing?
            ... You're lucky to be alive ...

EDWARD: (*Turning; furious*) And so's Mr Morris! If
            that blasted telephone hadn't rung I'd have
            killed him. (*Quietly, after a pause*) He
            murdered Fay ... I know that now ...
            there's no doubt in my mind ... As soon as
            I showed him the book, I knew damn well
            that ...

YATES: (*Interrupting him*) What book?

132

EDWARD: Fay had a book of poems … She'd obviously borrowed it from Morris; it had his name in it …

YATES: (*Intensely angry*) You stupid, idiotic fool! Why didn't you bring me that book?

EDWARD: Because I only found it the other day and you'd have done damn all about it anyway.

YATES: Well, at least, I wouldn't have lost it, Mr Collins!

EDWARD looks at YATES; angry and still a little dazed. Suddenly he sways and sinks into the armchair by the drinks table.

EDWARD: (*Quietly; hesitantly*) Do you think you could get me a drink? I feel pretty foul.

YATES: (*Turning towards the telephone*) You'd better see a doctor.

EDWARD: No, I don't want a doctor. I want a drink.

YATES looks at EDWARD, then crosses to the drinks table.

YATES: What would you like – brandy?

EDWARD nods and YATES pours the drink into a glass, then takes it to him. There is a pause. YATES watches EDWARD drink the brandy.

YATES: Where's your housekeeper?

EDWARD: She's gone – she left me days ago …

There is another pause. YATES still looks at EDWARD.

YATES: What is it you want, Collins? What are you after?

EDWARD looks up.

EDWARD: Clifton Morris murdered Fay … You've got to arrest him.

YATES: We can't – not yet, we haven't got sufficient proof.

133

EDWARD: Well, get it!

YATES looks at EDWARD, then gets hold of a chair and pulls it up to where he is sitting. YATES sits in the chair and leans forward.

YATES: (*Quietly*) Would you help me to get it, Mr Collins?

EDWARD looks at YATES, surprised by the question.

EDWARD: Why, yes …

YATES: Are you sure about that?

EDWARD: Yes … Yes, I'm quite sure.

There is a pause. YATES still looks at EDWARD, hesitant, undecided about something: then suddenly he makes up his mind and gives a decisive nod.

YATES: All right. Now this is what I want you to do …

CUT TO: The Drawing Room of CLIFTON MORRIS' Flat. Night.

CLIFTON MORRIS is standing by the open bookcase. He wears his outdoor clothes – having just returned from his interview with EDWARD – and looks tense and agitated. He puts the book of poems on the shelf. Suddenly the front doorbell rings, and MORRIS looks towards the hall. The bell rings again. MORRIS consults his watch, then quickly goes into the bedroom and returns a few seconds later without his hat and coat. He heads towards the hall.

CUT TO: The Hall of CLIFTON MORRIS' Flat. Night.

MORRIS opens the front door. A TELEGRAPH BOY stands in the doorway.

BOY: Mr Morris?

MORRIS: Yes.

The BOY hands MORRIS a telegram and goes. MORRIS closes the door and returns to the drawing room, opening the telegram as he does so. He reads it. It reads: "Must see you tonight. Kim".

CUT TO: The flashing neon sign advertising The Take-Off Club.

CUT TO: A Corridor of The Take-Off Club. Night.
Showgirls and various stage personnel are passing to and fro down the corridor. Music and Laughter can be heard from the stage.

HECTOR suddenly appears, rushing down the corridor, carrying a pile of girls' dresses, stockings, etc. He disappears into a dressing room. The number finishes on stage and there is a roar of applause. Several girls appear and go into various dressing rooms. KIM STEVENS can be seen at the end of the corridor. As she walks down it, HECTOR appears from the dressing room.
HECTOR: They're a bit lively tonight.
KIM: You can say that again!
HECTOR: (*Nodding towards KIM's dressing room*) Your
            boyfriend's here – he's been waiting half an
            hour.
KIM nods and goes into her dressing room.

CUT TO: KIM STEVENS' Dressing Room. Night.
KIM enters the room. She stops dead; staring across the dressing room. YATES is sprawled out in the armchair, waiting for KIM. He smiles and lifts his hand in a gesture of welcome.
YATES: Hi!
KIM stares at YATES in surprise. She is obviously frightened.

END OF EPISODE FOUR

EPISODE FIVE

OPEN TO: KIM STEVENS' Dressing Room. Night.

KIM enters the dressing room. She stops dead; staring across the room. YATES is sprawled out in the armchair, waiting for KIM. He smiles and lifts his hand in a gesture of welcome.

YATES: Hi!

KIM stares at YATES in surprise; obviously frightened.

KIM: What are you doing here?

YATES: I'm waiting for you, Kim. I've been waiting half-an-hour.

KIM: (*Crossing to the make-up table*) I'm in a hurry, I can't stop now, I'm on again in three minutes.

YATES: (*Shaking his head*) you've got nine minutes and no change – I've checked with Hector.

KIM: (*At the table; using powder*) Hector? He doesn't know whether it's Easter or Christmas! What is it   you want?

YATES: How's Dad?

KIM: (*Turning, looking at YATES, hesitantly*) He's all right, I think. At least he was the last time … Oh, God, is he in trouble again?

YATES: No; he's all right, he's doing very nicely for himself. It's his daughter I'm worried about.

KIM: You look worried!

YATES: I am, Kim – very worried. (*Touching his head*) I've got a neat little filing system up there, it always worries me when things go wrong with it.

KIM: What are you getting at?

YATES: I had you down under 'B' for bed – not 'B' for blackmail. You should tell me when you make these switches, Sweetie.

KIM: (*Annoyed*) What the hell are you talking about?

YATES: Clifton Morris.

139

KIM: (*Tensely*) Clifton Morris?

YATES: Yes. Is he a friend of yours?

KIM: (*A momentary hesitation, then a quick decision*) Yes; he is – we're very good friends. He's been here several times.

YATES: How long have you known Morris?

KIM: About a fortnight. He's supplying the caviar this month. (*Showing YATES a ring she is wearing*) He gave me this ruby ring.

YATES: That's not so hot. You should see the diamond bracelet he gave Fay Collins. (*Shaking his head*) I don't think he gave you that. I don't think he's the current boyfriend, either.

KIM: Well, what the hell do you think?

YATES: I've told you. I think you're blackmailing him.

YATES picks up a stocking from the dressing table and looks at it.

YATES: Kim, we've known one another quite a while now, haven't we? Do you remember the first time we met – in that restaurant in Tenby Street?

KIM: Restaurant? What a dump! They paid me a tenner a week and I did six numbers.

YATES: Yes, and damn good you were, too. (*Looking at the stocking*) Do you remember what I told you then?

KIM: (*Turning towards the mirror*) Yes, I had a record made of it.

YATES: Well, I should play it occasionally.

YATES stands behind KIM; close to her, looking down at her shoulders, still holding the stocking.

YATES: What are you trying to sell Morris?

KIM: I'm not trying to sell him anything. He's just a load of fun. You know these wealthy characters; they like to play around.

YATES: Not Clifton Morris. He's the serious type.

KIM: (*A laugh*) You don't know Cliff!

YATES: (*Quietly*) His friends don't call him Cliff – they call him Terry.

KIM: Well, I call him Cliff!

YATES: Kim, what is it? Who are you working for? What are you trying to sell Morris?

KIM: (*Turning*) Look, you're on the wrong track. I've told you – Cliff's just like all the other characters around here. He wants fun without being involved. Now be a darling, Harry – don't break this up. This is the jackpot; he's loaded.

YATES looks at KIM; there is a long pause. It is difficult to tell whether he believes her or not.

YATES: How much money have you got?

KIM: (*Surprised by the question*) What do you mean?

YATES: I'm asking you – how much money have you got?

KIM: (*Looking at YATES; curious*) I'm all right. I can get by.

YATES: Well, take a trip. Go to Paris – Rome – Naples – anywhere but take a trip.

KIM: What, now?

YATES: Yes, now – tonight – straight away.

KIM: (*Nervously; but with a little laugh*) What is this? What are you getting at?

YATES: Do you really want to know, Kim?

KIM: Yes.

YATES: I don't want you to finish up with a scarf round
           your neck.

*YATES drapes the stocking round KIM's shoulders and
walks out of the room. KIM stares after him; worried and
thoughtful; gently touching her throat.*

CUT TO: A corridor in The Take-Off Club. Night.

*YATES appears and walks down the corridor. A scantily
dressed young lady is speaking on the wall telephone.*

GIRL: … You can go to fifty lawyers but you're not
           getting the mink coat back …
YATES: (*As he passes the GIRL*) I hope you've reversed
           the charges …

CUT TO: The Drawing Room of CLIFTON MORRIS's
Flat. Night.

*The telephone is ringing. CLIFTON MORRIS comes
quickly out of the bedroom and answers it. He is on edge,
his manner tense. For the duration of this conversation, we
cut back and forth between MORRIS and KIM in the
corridor of The Take-Off Club using the wall telephone.*

MORRIS: (*On the phone*) Hello? …
KIM: (*On the other end of the line*) Mr Morris? This
           is Kim Stevens …
MORRIS: Look – I'm sorry I didn't see you tonight, but
           just as I got to Helston Street, I saw …
KIM: (*Tensely*) Wait a minute, Sweetie! Please …
MORRIS: What is it? What's happened?
KIM: A man called Yates came to see me. He's a
           Police Inspector …
MORRIS: (*Quickly*) Yes, I know. I saw him, that's why I
           didn't keep the appointment.

142

KIM: Now listen – I didn't tell him anything. I didn't
            mention Fay Collins, the letter, or anything.
            You understand.

MORRIS: Yes, I understand.

KIM: I'll see you later. I'll drop in about half past
            two – if that's all right?

The doorbell in CLIFTON MORRIS' flat begins ringing.

MORRIS: Yes, that's all right … But wait a minute!
            (*Quickly, quietly*) Look, what else did you tell
            Yates? I think he's here now …

KIM: I said you were the current boyfriend. You've
            given me a ring. I call you Cliff …

MORRIS: All right … I'll see you later.

MORRIS replaces the telephone receiver.

CUT TO: The Front Door of CLIFTON MORRIS' Flat.
Night.

*YATES is standing at the door, his finger on the bell. After
a moment, the door is opened by MORRIS who is
apparently surprised to see YATES there.*

MORRIS: Oh, hello, Inspector …

YATES: Good evening, sir. Can you spare me a few
            minutes?

MORRIS: Yes – come in …

CUT TO: The Drawing Room of the flat. Night.

YATES enters, followed by MORRIS.

YATES: Mr Morris, why on earth didn't you tell us that
            you'd been to The Take-Off Club last night?

MORRIS: I don't know why. It was stupid of me. (*He
            crosses to the drinks table*) I nearly telephoned
            you about it this morning, but … (*A shrug*) I

143

suppose I just didn't want to advertise the fact that I'd been there.

YATES: I suggest you had another reason for not telling me.

MORRIS: What do you mean?

YATES: I suggest you didn't want us to know why you visited Miss Stevens.

MORRIS: Now, don't be silly! Why does anyone ever visit a place like The Take-Off Club? (*A shrug*) Kim's a girl friend of mine – we have fun together. That's all there is to it.

YATES: I find that difficult to believe, sir.

MORRIS: You don't know Kim Stevens.

YATES: On the contrary, I know her extremely well. I've known her for years. How long have you known her, Mr Morris?

MORRIS: About – about three weeks.

YATES: I see. (*After a moment*) Kim showed me a diamond ring you'd given her.

MORRIS: Well?

YATES: Do you usually give diamond rings to young ladies you've only known for three weeks?

MORRIS: That rather depends. When they're as pleasant as Kim – yes, Inspector. (*Annoyed*) Look, why exactly did you come here tonight?

YATES: Because I didn't get anywhere with Kim. She told me you were a boyfriend of hers – the latest popsie. (*Shaking his head*) I didn't believe her.

MORRIS: You don't seem to believe anything, Inspector.

YATES: I believe what I see, sir.

MORRIS: What do you mean?

YATES: You don't look like a popsie, and I'm quite sure you know the difference between a diamond and a ruby. It was a ruby ring she showed me, Mr Morris.

MORRIS: (*Irritated, turning away from the table*) Have you got any other tricks up your sleeve, Inspector?

YATES: Not at the moment, sir, but I'm working on them. (*Moving towards MORRIS*) Last time I was here I asked you about Fay Collins.

MORRIS: (*Turning*) You've never stopped asking me about her!

YATES: Well, here's a new one, sir. Is her brother a friend of yours?

MORRIS: I don't expect you to believe me, but the answer's no.

YATES: There's no reason why I shouldn't believe you, sir. (*He turns away and crosses towards the hall*) I'm sorry you won't tell me why you went to see Kim. It might have simplified matters.

MORRIS: I've told you why I went to see her! (*A shrug*) Good God, Inspector, you're a man of the world! We can't all play golf!

YATES: (*With the suggestion of a smile*) Goodnight, Mr Morris.

YATES goes out into the hall. MORRIS hesitates, then suddenly follows him.

CUT TO: The Hall of CLIFTON MORRIS's Flat.

MORRIS: (*Coming out of the drawing room*) Wait a minute, Inspector!

YATES turns and looks at MORRIS.

MORRIS: Why did you ask me if I knew Edward Collins?

YATES: Someone broke into his house the other day and he was badly hurt – he's in the local hospital.

MORRIS: (*Quietly astonished*) What do you mean – badly hurt?

YATES: Well, he's unconscious – on the danger list.

MORRIS: Have you any idea what happened – who did it?

YATES: (*Casually*) No, we haven't. There's been quite a few robberies round Littleshaw just lately. We think probably someone broke into the house and Collins disturbed him. The housekeeper was out. When she got back Collins was on the floor. We'll know more, of course, if he regains consciousness.

MORRIS: If he regains consciousness?

YATES: Yes. (*Nodding*) Oh, he's pretty bad, I'm afraid. (*He turns towards the door*) Goodnight, sir. (*He opens the door and goes out*)

MORRIS stands in the hall, obviously shocked by the news about EDWARD. He looks distinctly worried as he turns towards the drawing room.

CUT TO: The Exterior of a block of flats in Mayfair in which CLIFTON MORRIS has his flat. About 3 o'clock in the morning.

A taxi drives up to the block of flats and KIM STEVENS gets out, and after quickly paying the driver, hurries into the main entrance.

CUT TO: A corridor in the block of flats.

KIM arrives at the front door of MORRIS's flat. She presses the bell and stands waiting. After a moment the door is opened by CLIFTON MORRIS, who is now wearing a dressing gown. KIM enters the flat.

CUT TO: The Drawing Room of CLIFTON MORRIS's Flat.

KIM enters, followed by MORRIS.

KIM: (*A shade breathless*) I'm sorry I'm late. We didn't get away until three, and I couldn't get a taxi for love or money.

MORRIS: Would you like a drink?

KIM: No. (*Tensely*) What happened tonight – did you see Yates? Did you tell him about the letter?

MORRIS: Of course I didn't.

KIM: (*Nervously*) Are you sure?

MORRIS: My dear Kim, if I was prepared to tell Yates about the letter, I shouldn't have come to you in the first place – and you wouldn't be blackmailing me.

KIM: (*Annoyed*) I'm not blackmailing you!

MORRIS: Then who is?

KIM: (*Hesitant; nervously*) That's what I wanted to talk to you about. I – I made a mistake. I can't get you that letter after all.

MORRIS: (*Taking hold of KIM's arm*) You've got to get it! Now that Diana Winston's dead it's more important than ever.

KIM: (*Releasing herself*) Yes, I know but – well, I'm sorry, there's nothing I can do about it.

MORRIS: If it's a question of money …

KIM: No. No, it isn't – it's nothing to do with the money, it's just that – well … (*Shaking her head*)   … I can't get it.

MORRIS: You told me you could. You told me that if I paid …

KIM: (*Interrupting him; tensely*) I know what I told you, and I've changed my mind.

MORRIS: Who's got that letter?

KIM: I don't know.

MORRIS: You must know!

KIM: I don't …

MORRIS: Then how did you hear about it in the first place?

KIM: (*Hesitantly*) Someone I know told me about it. They asked me to contact you – to act as a go-between. They said if I did, I'd get two hundred pounds …

MORRIS: Who was this someone?

KIM: A woman – a friend of mine.

MORRIS: All right. Just tell this friend of yours to get in touch with me.

KIM: I don't think she'd do that. In fact, I'm sure she wouldn't …

MORRIS: Well, try … ask her.

KIM: Well … (*Looking at MORRIS*) … If I do, will you do me a favour?

MORRIS: I might.

KIM: Will you promise not to tell Yates what really happened between us?

MORRIS: I haven't the slightest intention of telling him what happened, so don't worry about that.

KIM: All right then. I'll phone my friend tomorrow morning.

MORRIS: Thank you. (*With the suggestion of a smile*) Now will you change your mind about the drink?

KIM: I'll have a brandy – a double.

MORRIS: (*Looking at KIM; smiling*) Yates really scared you, didn't he, Sweetie?

KIM: He scared the pants off me!

CUT TO: YATES's Office at Littleshaw Police Station. Morning.

MARIAN HASTINGS in sitting in an armchair. She looks annoyed and irritated. After a moment she rises and takes a cigarette case out of her handbag; she is about to light the cigarette when YATES comes into the office carrying a folder of documents.

YATES: I'm sorry to have kept you waiting, Miss Hastings.

MARIAN: (*Replacing the cigarette case and cigarette in her handbag*) Look here, Inspector – I've been sitting here for fifteen minutes! What's this all about?

YATES sits at the desk and opens the folder.

YATES: I want to have a talk to you.

MARIAN: Well, I didn't think you'd invited me for coffee!

As MARIAN speaks, PC KENT comes into the office with a cup of coffee which he puts down on the desk and then goes back out.

YATES: (*To MARIAN; excessively politely*) Would you like a cup of coffee, Miss Hastings?

MARIAN: No, I wouldn't. I'm an extremely busy woman, so if you've got anything to say to me, I'd be grateful if you'd say it.

149

YATES: Right. (*He points to the folder*) I've checked this hotel at Chamonix; it's owned by an English woman called Mrs Browning. She's a friend of yours.

MARIAN: (*Hesitantly*) Yes …

YATES: She's confirmed your story, but quite frankly, I don't believe her. (*He rises*) I want to see your passport.

MARIAN: Are you suggesting I'm a liar, then?

YATES: I'm simply suggesting that you didn't go to Chamonix. If you don't show me your passport, I'll check with Passport Control. It's entirely up to you.

There is a pause. MARIAN looks at YATES; undecided about what to do.

YATES: Well? (*Another pause*) Well, Miss Hastings?

MARIAN: (*Turning away from YATES; looking out of the window*) You're quite right, I didn't go to Chamonix. I was in London.

YATES: Then obviously you read about the murder the morning after it happened.

MARIAN: Yes.

YATES: Why didn't you get in touch with us straight away?

MARIAN: Because my fiancé thought I was abroad and I – I didn't want to disillusion him.

YATES: There was no need to disillusion him – you could have told him you'd just flown back from Geneva.

MARIAN: He knows I hate flying. He wouldn't have believed me.

YATES: What were you doing in London, anyway?

MARIAN: That's my business.

YATES: It is indeed, Miss Hastings, but it also
            happens to be my business at the moment.

MARIAN: I refuse to answer such an impertinent
            question!

YATES: I'm afraid you'll have to answer it sooner
            or later. (*Politely*) You know we're not
            interested in your relationship with Mr
            Goodman. If you've got a boyfriend in
            Town, it's no concern of …

MARIAN: How dare you! I've a very good mind to
            report you to your superior!

YATES: (*Unperturbed*) It's an excellent idea –
            unless you've got someone in mind, may I
            suggest Superintendent Nash? I'm sure
            he'd be delighted to have a talk with you.

*MARIAN glares at YATES, then picks up her handbag
from the desk.*

MARIAN: I think we're wasting each other's time,
            Inspector. Good morning …

*JEFFREYS opens the door and enters, and MARIAN goes
out.*

YATES: (*Bringing his fist down on the table*) That
            … (*Restraining himself from using the
            word 'bloody'*) … confounded woman.

JEFFREYS: What's happened?

YATES: Matthews was right. She was in London –
            she never went to Chamonix.

JEFFREYS: Then why did she wait several days before
telling   us about Morris?

YATES: Don't you know why?

JEFFREYS: (*Puzzled*) No.

YATES: (*After a moment*) She was told to wait.

JEFFREYS: Told to wait?

YATES: Yes.

JEFFREYS: By whom?

YATES: (*Looking at JEFFREYS; quietly*) Yes, that's the question, Jeff. By whom …? (*He picks up a letter from the folder on his desk*) Did you see this from the insurance company?

JEFFREYS: No?

YATES: It's about the diamond bracelet. Someone insured it for a thousand pounds, just over twelve months ago. Do you know who it was?

JEFFREYS: No.

YATES: Fay Collins …

JEFFREYS: (*Astonished*) Fay? But she couldn't have done! Why dammit, she never received it! She was dead before … (*He stops; looks at YATES*) You mean that bracelet actually belonged to Fay Collins?

YATES: That's exactly what I mean. (*Putting down the letter*) Someone took that bracelet from her flat, put the note in it about Le Lavencher, and posted it to her; knowing perfectly well, that by the time it arrived here, she'd be dead.

JEFFREYS: Then you don't think that Morris sent her the bracelet?

YATES: (*Shaking his head*) No, I don't – that's what we were meant to think.

JEFFREYS: He wrote the note …

YATES: Yes, he wrote the note, and at some time or another he sent it to someone – possibly to Fay – but he didn't send it with a diamond bracelet, I'm sure of that.

JEFFREYS: I get it. You mean that note belonged to a
               bunch of flowers, or a box of chocolates,
               or possibly …

PC KENT enters.

YATES: (*Interrupting JEFFREYS*) Exactly!
               (*Turning towards KENT*) Yes, what is it?

KENT: Mr Hopedean's here, sir. He'd like a word
               with you.

YATES: All right. Send him in …

*JEFFREYS crosses and picks up the insurance letter from
the desk.*

JEFFREYS: (*Looking at the letter*) Then you don't
               think Morris murdered Fay Collins?

YATES: (*Quietly*) I didn't say that. I just said he
               didn't send her the bracelet …

*JOHN HOPEDEAN enters. He carries a very large cloth-
bound folder, as used by artists for carrying art proofs,
illustrations, etc.*

YATES: (*To HOPEDEAN*) Good morning, sir. You
               know Sergeant Jeffreys?

HOPEDEAN: Yes, of course.

JEFFREYS: Good morning, Mr Hopedean.

HOPEDEAN: Hello, Sergeant …

YATES: Do sit down, sir. (*He moves behind the
               desk*)

HOPEDEAN: No, I won't keep you a moment, Inspector;
               it's just that I've got some news which I
               thought might interest you.

YATES: (*Pleasantly*) Well, you might as well sit
               down, sir …

HOPEDEAN: Oh, well – thank you. (*He sits in the
               armchair: putting the folder down by the
               desk*) Inspector, I've been up to Fleet
               Street this morning, delivering some

153

material, and I bumped into a friend of mine called Finchley. Awfully nice chap; he's on the Weekly spotlight.

JEFFREYS: Isn't that one of Clifton Morris's magazines?

HOPEDEAN: That's right, Sergeant. Well, apparently Finchley knew Diana Weston quite well, and actually bumped into her about four or five hours before she was murdered.

YATES: Where?

HOPEDEAN: I think he said in the Carlton Hotel, but I'm not sure – anyway wherever it was, they had a drink together.

YATES: Go on …

HOPEDEAN: Well, according to Finchley, she was in very high spirits – absolutely elated. She told him she'd just landed the most wonderful job with Clifton Morris.

YATES: Did she say what it was?

HOPEDEAN: Yes. Apparently, she was going out to Rome to work on a fashion magazine – or start a magazine, or something like that. Anyway, she was terribly excited about it.

YATES: Did this friend of yours say anything else about Miss Winston?

HOPEDEAN: No, that's all, and it doesn't amount to much, I admit, but I thought out of fairness to Mr Morris you ought to hear about it.

YATES: I don't quite follow you, sir?

HOPEDEAN: Well, I don't know a great deal about this case, of course – in fact, only what I've read in the newspapers – but everybody seems to think Morris did it. But if Finchley is telling the truth – he obviously

154

is – then Morris couldn't have done it. I mean, you don't offer a girl a jolly good job one minute, and murder her the next, now do you?

YATES: (*Smiling*) No, sir. Thank you, Mr Hopedean. I take it this friend of yours will corroborate his story.

HOPEDEAN: Why yes, of course. He's in the book. P.J. Finchley – Palmer's Green. (*To JEFFREYS: picking up his folder*) Goodbye, Sergeant.

JEFFREYS: Goodbye, sir.

YATES goes out with HOPEDEAN. JEFFREYS crosses and stands by the window; he turns as YATES comes back into the room.

JEFFREYS: Harry, do you think Morris offered her the Italian job as a bribe – in exchange for an alibi?

YATES looks at JEFFREYS but makes no comment.

JEFFREYS: The thought had occurred to you, of course?

YATES: Oh, yes. (*He looks towards the door*) I'm just wondering if it had occurred to Mr Hopedean …

CUT TO: KIM STEVENS' Bedroom. Day.

This is a small, but essentially feminine, room, somewhat theatrical in personality. KIM is standing, packing clothes into an open suitcase. There is another suitcase, obviously already packed, on the floor near the door. A telephone and radio stand on a table by the side of the ornate bed. Several dresses, coats, etc, are on the bed.

The telephone rings and KIM turns and picks up the receiver.

KIM: (*On the phone*) Hello? …

PBX OPERATOR: (*On the other end of the phone*) I've got your Mayfair number now …

KIM: Thank you …

PBX OPERATOR: (*On the phone*) Clifton Morris Publications   …

KIM: I want to speak to Mr Morris, please.

PBX OPERATOR: I'm very sorry, but Mr Morris can't be disturbed …

KIM: (*Annoyed*) Look, I've been trying to get Mr Morris all morning. My name's Kim Stevens. Put me through!

PBX OPERATOR: One moment, please …

CUT TO: A corner of CLIFTON MORRIS' Office. Day. This corner is occupied almost completely by a section of a very large desk. We see several telephones: a Dictaphone: internal speakers etc.

MORRIS is standing by the desk, reading a balance sheet. The telephone rings and he picks up one of the receivers.

PBX OPERATOR: I'm sorry to disturb you, sir, but there's a Miss Stevens on the line, and she absolutely insists …

MORRIS: (*Interrupting her*) Put her on.

KIM: (*On the other end of the line*) Hello? …

MORRIS: Kim? …

KIM: My hat, are you difficult to get! I've been trying all morning!

MORRIS: I'm sorry. (*Quietly*) Have you got any news for me?

156

CUT TO: KIM STEVENS' Bedroom. Day.

KIM is speaking on the telephone.

KIM: Yes; I've spoken to my friend. Someone's
                going to get in touch with you …

MORRIS: (*On the other end*) When?

KIM: I don't know when – perhaps tonight – I'm
                not sure.

MORRIS: All right, Kim. Thank you very much.
                Good luck …

KIM: If you ever get to Paris – look me up,
                Sweetie.

*KIM replaces the receiver. She turns and picks up a dress
from off the bed. She holds it up, about to fold it ready for
the suitcase.*

CUT TO: MARIAN HASTINGS' Dress Shop. Day.

*MARIAN is holding a dress and PHYLLIS is pinning up
the hem in an attempt to shorten it.*

PHYLLIS: That's all right, Miss Hastings. I think I
                can manage now.

MARIAN puts the dress down on the table.

MARIAN: How long do you think it'll take, Phyllis?

PHYLLIS: With a bit of luck, it should be ready in
                about an hour.

MARIAN: Oh, good. I said she could have it by three
                o'clock.

*The doorbell sounds and ALISTAIR GOODMAN enters.
He carries a hat box.*

MARIAN: (*Turning: surprised*) Oh, hello, Alistair!

GOODMAN: Hello, my dear! How are you, Phyllis?

PHYLLIS: I'm very well, thank you, Mr Goodman.

*PHYLLIS pulls a chair up to the table and proceeds to
make the alteration to the dress.*

157

GOODMAN: (*Putting down the hat box*) With Mrs Baxter's compliments – she'll be popping in to see you!

MARIAN: (*Opening the box and taking out a hat*) Good Lord, she only bought the wretched thing this morning!

GOODMAN: She's decided it doesn't suit her after all.

MARIAN: Of course it doesn't suit her! Nothing suits her! She looks like a horse!

GOODMAN: Well, sell her a bridle, Duckie. Most extraordinary woman – every time she sees me she makes me deliver something. (*With a laugh*) Probably thinks I'm the District Nurse.

PHYLLIS laughs.

MARIAN: Well, are you going to take me out to lunch, Alistair?

GOODMAN: No, dear, I can't. I've got the Milk Board people at two o'clock. (*Curious*) Marian, didn't I see you coming out of the police station this morning?

MARIAN: Yes, the Inspector wanted to have a word with me.

GOODMAN: What about?

MARIAN: Oh, nothing, Alistair.

GOODMAN: Well, it must have been about something.

MARIAN: (*With a glance at PHYLLIS*) He wanted to have another talk about Fay Collins.

GOODMAN: Good Lord, he's always talking to you about Fay Collins. What was it this time?

MARIAN looks at GOODMAN, then nods towards PHYLLIS, who is busy on the dress.

MARIAN: I'll tell you tonight, Alistair.

158

GOODMAN looks at MARIAN, quite serious for a moment, then gives a little nod.

GOODMAN: All right, old girl. (*Brightly: to PHYLLIS*) Be good, Phyllis! Remember what your mother told you.

GOODMAN kisses MARIAN and goes out. MARIAN looks towards the door, then turns and picks up the hat box.

CUT TO: MARIAN HASTINGS' Office in the Dress Shop. About an hour later.

MARIAN is sitting at a tiny bureau, writing a letter. Her hat and gloves are on the top of the bureau. After a moment, PHYLLIS appears in the open doorway, with a dress box.

PHYLLIS: It's ready, Miss Hastings.

MARIAN: (*Turning*) Oh, thank you, Phyllis.

MARIAN rises, puts the unfinished letter in a drawer and then puts on her hat and gloves.

CUT TO: The Dress Shop. Day.

MARIAN joins PHYLLIS and takes the box from her.

MARIAN: I'll be back in about an hour, then you can get off.

PHYLLIS: (*Smiling*) There's no hurry, I'm not meeting David till five o'clock.

MARIAN nods and goes out. PHYLLIS crosses down to the table and begins to collect her various odds and ends. Finally, she picks up the sewing basket and crosses towards the office. Suddenly, from outside the shop, there is the sound of a car racing past the window, followed by revolver shots, and the smashing of glass. We hear a terrified shriek from MARIAN HASTINGS. PHYLLIS

159

stands, horrified, looking towards the door. Suddenly she drops her sewing basket and runs out of the shop.

CUT TO: The Main Street at Littleshaw. Day.

PHYLLIS comes running out of the dress shop. MARIAN is leaning against the open door of her car, holding on to it for support. The windscreen of the car has been shattered by bullets. MARIAN is trembling with fear but, except for a cut on her hand, is apparently unhurt. Several people are converging on the scene from various points. GERALD QUINCEY reaches MARIAN just before PHYLLIS arrives.

GERALD: (*Taking hold of MARIAN's arm*) Are you all right?

MARIAN: (*Dazed*) Yes … I think so …

GERALD: Your hand's cut …

MARIAN: (*Faintly: nodding*) It's nothing … it's probably a piece of glass from the windscreen …

Several people have now arrived on the scene, including PHYLLIS, and are crowding round MARIAN.

PHYLLIS: *(To GERALD)* What happened?

GERALD: Someone fired at her from a passing car. I thought at first it was …

PHYLLIS: (*Quickly*) She's fainting!

GERALD turns and catches MARIAN as she faints.

CUT TO: The Office in MARIAN's Dress Shop. Day.

MARIAN is sitting in the armchair. PHYLLIS is kneeling by her side, bathing the injured hand in a bowl of water. GERALD QUINCEY stands near the table, looking down at MARIAN.

MARIAN: It's perfectly all right, Phyllis – please don't fuss …

160

PHYLLIS: (*Rising*) Are you sure, Miss Hastings?

MARIAN: Yes, I'm quite sure – thank you, Phyllis. (*To GERALD*) Did you see the car?

GERALD: Yes, I did; but I didn't take much notice of it – I thought at first it was just backfiring.

MARIAN: (*Nodding*) Yes, I know. (*A moment; hesitant*) You didn't recognise the driver, I suppose?

The sound of a police car drawing to a standstill outside the shop is heard.

GERALD: No, and I don't think anyone else would, either.

MARIAN: Why?

GERALD: His hat was pulled down and he was wearing dark glasses.

MARIAN looks at GERALD, then gives a little nod and looks down at her hand. GERALD turns towards the door.

GERALD: Here's the police, Miss Hastings ...

CUT TO: London Airport. The Main Hall with an escalator in the foreground.

YATES walks towards the escalator. He wears a light overcoat and carries a folded newspaper under his arm. He travels up the escalator towards the balcony and the restaurant lounge.

CUT TO: London Airport.

YATES is standing in the lounge, obviously looking for someone. Suddenly he notices the person he is looking for and, with a little smile, crosses out of picture.

161

CUT TO: A corner table in a lounge at London Airport. Day.

KIM is sitting on a settee, in front of a low table, smoking a cigarette. There is a travel bag by her side. After a moment she looks up and with a start of surprise, recognises YATES. YATES appears and sits in the vacant chair.

YATES: (*Pleasantly*) Hello, Kim!

KIM: What do you want?

YATES: I came to congratulate you. I didn't think you had the sense to take my advice.

KIM: I don't know what you're talking about. I've been overworking. I need a holiday. I'll be back at the end of the week.

YATES: Not if you've got any sense, you won't. (*He opens his newspaper and puts it down on the table*) Have you seen this?

KIM looks at YATES; then down at the newspaper on the front page of which is a photograph of MARIAN's car with the shattered windscreen; also of the dress shop, with an insert photograph of MARIAN herself. The headline reads: 'Shots in Littleshaw Street – Attempted Murder'. KIM stares at the newspaper; she looks up at YATES and gives a little nod.

KIM: Yes; I've seen it.

YATES: (*Pointing to the newspaper*) She's a friend of yours, isn't she?

KIM: No …

YATES: (*Quietly*) Come on, Kim. Come off it!

KIM: (*Tensely*) I've never seen the woman. I don't know anything about this.

YATES: Are you sure?

KIM: Of course I'm sure! Do you think I don't know who my friends are?

YATES: Oh, well this puts rather a different complexion on things. I thought she <u>was</u> a friend of yours. (*He looks at his watch*) Collect your things, we're going back to Town.

KIM: (*Amazed*) What do you mean? What are you talking about?

YATES: (*Leaning towards KIM*) Kim, I want certain information about Marian Hastings. I think you can give it to me. If you can't – or you won't – okay – then I'll get it from somebody else. (*Shaking his head*) But you're not leaving this town until I do get it.

KIM: (*Frightened*) You're joking, Harry. You wouldn't do that.

YATES: Oh, yes I would.

KIM looks at YATES; worried and undecided. YATES looks at his watch again, then at KIM.

YATES: Well, it's up to you.

KIM: All right … All right, Harry. (*She stubs out her cigarette in the ashtray*) I didn't know what I was letting myself in for. I've known this woman – Marian Hastings – about six months …

YATES: Go on …

KIM: She asked me to get in touch with Morris – to act as a go-between. She said a friend of hers had a letter which Morris wanted – it was a letter he'd written to Fay Collins.

YATES: Did she tell you who this friend of hers was?

KIM: No, she didn't, but she's terrified of him, really terrified. I think he's the man who murdered Fay   …

163

YATES:	(*Quietly, watching KIM*) Yes, so do I, Kim.
KIM:	(*Looking at YATES, alarmed*) Harry, I don't know who he is. Honestly, I don't …
YATES:	Don't you, Kim?
KIM:	(*Shaking her head*) No, I don't … I swear to you, Harry … Honestly, I don't …

There is a pause. YATES looks at KIM; he looks very serious.

YATES:	All right – you don't know. (*With the beginning of a smile*) But I do, Sweetie. (*He takes out his cigarette case, and offers her a cigarette*) Now tell me the rest of this story …

CUT TO: YATES' Office at Littleshaw Police Station. Night.

JEFFREYS is sitting in YATES's chair behind the desk. He takes a cigarette out of a cigarette case and he is lighting it as PC KENT enters with a cup of coffee.

KENT:	Fred's just been making some coffee; we thought you'd like a cup.
JEFFREYS:	No thanks. Does Fred do anything else, except make coffee?
KENT:	He's very good on tea.
JEFFREYS:	(*Smiling*) All right, put it down. (*He looks at his watch*) The Inspector said half past six?
KENT:	Half past six, on the dot.
JEFFREYS:	(*Nodding*) Right! (*He turns and picks up the phone and starts to dial a number*)

CUT TO: The Drawing Room of CLIFTON MORRIS' Flat. Night.

MORRIS is standing by the fireplace, facing YATES. He looks distinctly irritated.

MORRIS: … Perhaps I've got a one-track mind, Inspector …

YATES: ... Oh, I wouldn't say that sir …

MORRIS: … But for the life of me, I can't imagine why you think I had anything to do with this business in Littleshaw.

YATES: I should have thought it was obvious, sir. Miss Hastings happens to be the person who saw you with Fay Collins.

MORRIS: Oh, I see. Light is beginning to dawn, at last. Miss Hastings says she saw me with Fay Collins, so naturally I've got to get rid of Miss Hastings.

YATES: Well, somebody tried to get rid of her, sir!

MORRIS: Well, it wasn't me, Inspector! (*He moves towards YATES*) When did you say this happened?

YATES: At about half past two this afternoon.

MORRIS: Well, from ten o'clock this morning, until approximately a quarter to four this afternoon I was at a Board Meeting, Inspector.

The telephone starts to ring.

YATES: It's a pity you didn't tell me that five minutes ago, sir.

MORRIS looks at YATES, then crosses to the telephone and answers it.

MORRIS: (*On the phone*) Hello?

JEFFREYS: (*On the other end of the phone*) Is that Mr
             Morris?
MORRIS: Yes, speaking …

CUT TO: YATES' Office.

JEFFREYS is sitting at the desk, on the telephone.
JEFFREYS: This is Sergeant Jeffreys – Littleshaw. Is
             Inspector Yates with you, by any chance,
             sir?
MORRIS: Yes, he is. Hold on …
JEFFREYS: Thank you, sir …

CUT TO: The Drawing Room.

MORRIS: (*To YATES*) It's for you.
YATES: (*Apparently surprised*) For me?
MORRIS: Yes.
YATES nods and takes the receiver from MORRIS.
MORRIS crosses to the drinks table and, turning his back
on YATES, starts to mix himself a drink.
YATES: (*On the phone*) Yates speaking …
JEFFREYS: (*On the other end*) This is Sergeant
             Jeffreys, sir. I'm sorry to bother you,
             Inspector, but we've just had some very
             bad news about Edward Collins.
YATES: What about Mr Collins?
MORRIS turns and looks across at YATES.
JEFFREYS: I'm afraid he's dead, sir.
YATES: Oh, dear – I'm sorry to hear that. When
             did he die, Sergeant?
JEFFREYS: The hospital telephoned about five
             minutes ago, sir.
YATES: All right, Jeff. I'll see you later.

YATES replaces the receiver. MORRIS puts down his glass and moves towards YATES; he is obviously staggered by the news.

YATES: Edward Collins is dead. The hospital have just telephoned us. He died this afternoon.

MORRIS: (*Softly*) Good God!

YATES: Well, if you'll excuse me, sir, I've got to get back to Littleshaw.

YATES picks up his hat from the settee, looks across at MORRIS, and then goes out into the hall leaving CLIFTON MORRIS looking bewildered and desperately worried.

CUT TO: The Drawing Room of CLIFTON MORRIS' Flat. Two hours later.

CLIFTON MORRIS comes out of the bedroom, wearing a dressing gown and carrying a glass of brandy. He crosses to the settee, picks up an ashtray which is full of cigarette ends off of it, and moves across to the drinks table. He is putting down the ashtray when the doorbell rings. He hesitates a moment, then turns and goes out into the hall.

CUT TO: The Hall of CLIFTON MORRIS' Flat. Night.

MORRIS comes out of the drawing room and crosses to the front door which he opens. The REVEREND NIGEL MATTHEWS is standing in the doorway.

MATTHEWS: Hello, Terry! (*Smiling*) I think you're expecting me …

END OF EPISODE FIVE

EPISODE SIX

OPEN TO: The Hall of CLIFTON MORRIS' Flat. Night.
*MORRIS is opening the front door. The REVEREND
NIGEL MATTHEWS is standing in the doorway.*

MATTHEWS: Hello, Terry! (*Smiling*) I think you're
expecting me …

MORRIS: (*Anxiously*) Yes … Yes, come in, Nigel.
It's awfully kind of you to come along at a
moment's notice like this; I do appreciate
it.

MATTHEWS: I was just going to a meeting when you
telephoned.

MORRIS: Oh, I'm sorry …

*MORRIS takes MATTHEWS by the arm and leads him
towards the drawing room.*

MATTHEWS: I'm not; I wanted to get out of it. Your
S.O.S. was an admirable excuse …

CUT TO: The Drawing Room of CLIFTON MORRIS'
Flat. Night.
MORRIS enters with MATTHEWS.

MATTHEWS: Now, what's this all about, Terry? You
sounded desperately worried on the
telephone.

*MORRIS indicates the armchair and MATTHEWS sits
down.*

MORRIS: Nigel, you know I'm mixed up in this
Collins case; you know the police think I
murdered her?

MATTHEWS: I only know what I've read in the
newspapers and what Inspector Yates has
told me.

MORRIS: Is Yates a friend of yours, then?

MATTHEWS: Yes, I think you could say he was a friend
of mine. I think he could be a friend of

171

yours too, Terry, if you were sensible enough to confide in him.

MORRIS: (*Shaking his head*) Yates doesn't believe me, he doesn't believe a word I say.

MATTHEWS: Is that entirely his fault?

MORRIS: (*Hesitating; turning away*) No. No, I suppose not. (*He turns again*) Would you like a drink, Nigel?

MATTHEWS: (*Smiling*) No, but I'd like to know why you sent for me?

MORRIS moves towards MATTHEWS.

MORRIS: (*Bluntly*) Do you think I murdered Fay Collins?

MATTHEWS: (*Looking at MORRIS*) No; but I've a shrewd suspicion that you knew her, that she was, in fact, a friend of yours.

MORRIS: (*Sitting on the arm of the settee; nodding*) Yes …

MATTHEWS: (*Quietly*) Terry, what happened, exactly? Tell me …

MORRIS: I met Fay Collins about six months ago. It was in a restaurant called Le Lavencher. I go there quite a lot; the food's awfully good and they have private little alcoves where you can talk business and – (*Looks at MATTHEWS*) … talk business.

MATTHEWS: Go on …

MORRIS: She told me her name was Fay Edwards, that she was a model, and that she supported her husband who was a polio victim. After we'd known each other about a month, she borrowed three hundred pounds from me. A fortnight later, she repaid it.

MATTHEWS: Go on …

MORRIS: The three hundred pounds, of course, was a bait; the old confidence trick. It crossed my mind at the time, but I just didn't want to think about it. Two weeks later she borrowed fifteen hundred pounds. (*He rises and walks to the drinks table*) Shortly after this happened, I had dinner with an Australian friend of mine, who comes over here about once a year. He told me that he knew Fay. He said her name was Collins; that she was unmarried; and that to say the least, she was a pretty expensive customer. I didn't believe him at first; I didn't believe him because …

MATTHEWS: You didn't want to …

MORRIS: (*Nodding*) Exactly. Anyway, I made one or two discreet enquiries, and it soon became pretty obvious that he'd been telling me the truth. I was furious; not only with Fay, of course, but with myself. I wrote her a letter – a pretty threatening letter, I'm afraid – demanding the immediate repayment of the fifteen hundred. She didn't reply, so I telephoned her.

MATTHEWS: Go on …

MORRIS: She asked me to meet her and talk things over. Like a fool, I agreed to do so. We arranged to meet on the night of January the 7th, in Littleshaw.

MATTHEWS: (*Rising*) But that was the night she was murdered.

MORRIS: Yes, I know.

173

MATTHEWS: Did you go down to Littleshaw, then – did you see her that night?

MORRIS: No; I intended to go. I actually got the car out and drove as far as Oakdene. (*A moment*) Then I changed my mind.

MATTHEWS: Why?

MORRIS: Because for the first time I realised I was out of my depth. I decided to forget Fay, and the fifteen hundred pounds. I drove back to Town, parked the car in Hyde Park, and went to the cinema in Curzon Street. Unfortunately, so far as I know, no one saw me. The next morning, I read about the murder.

MATTHEWS moves towards MORRIS.

MATTHEWS: Is that the truth, Terry?

MORRIS: The whole truth, Nigel – I swear it.

MATTHEWS: (*Smiling*) Then you've nothing to worry about.

MORRIS: (*Shaking his head; quietly*) Nothing – except Edward Collins.

MATTHEWS: (*Still smiling*) Well, I certainly wouldn't worry about Edward; he's perfectly all right.

MORRIS: What do you mean?

MATTHEWS: I'm afraid Yates took a leaf out of your book –and lied about Edward. You see, he was determined to get the truth out of you, Terry – one way or the other.

MORRIS: (*Relieved*) Well, I'm damned! (*Quite seriously; with enthusiasm*) You know, that fellow Yates is too good to be a copper – he ought to be working for me!

MATTHEWS laughs.

174

MORRIS: No, I'm serious, Nigel …

MATTHEWS: You don't know why I'm laughing. He wants you to work for him!

MORRIS: What do you mean?

MATTHEWS crosses to the settee and sits down.

MATTHEWS: (*Quietly*) Get me that drink, Terry – and I'll tell you.

MORRIS looks at MATTHEWS, then crosses to the drinks table. He mixes a whisky and soda for MATTHEWS, then one for himself. He picks up the two glasses and turns away from the table.

CUT TO: YATES' Office at Littleshaw Police Station. Day.

YATES is in his usual position behind the desk, listening to MATTHEWS, who is sitting in the armchair. JEFFREYS is on the left of the desk, facing both YATES and the PADRE.

MATTHEWS: … I told Terry that if only he'd told you the truth in the first place, he'd have saved himself a great deal of trouble, and would probably never have been suspected.

YATES: And what did he say?

MATTHEWS: I don't think he believed me.

YATES: (*Smiling*) I'm not surprised, sir. You see, Morris was suspected, not because he didn't tell the truth, but because everything pointed to the fact that he'd murdered Fay Collins.

MATTHEWS: Then why didn't you arrest him?

YATES: Because, fortunately for Mr Morris, there was a doubt in my mind. (*He rises; comes round the desk*) Padre, you've been very

175

helpful, and I think it only fair that I should satisfy your obvious curiosity.

MATTHEWS: Well, I must admit I am curious, Inspector – very curious. (*Smiling at JEFFREYS*) The trouble is, I'm not quite sure whether one should be …

YATES: Fay Collins worked for a blackmailer. Let's called him Mr A, shall we? Mr A suddenly decided to get rid of Fay and conceived the idea of murdering her, throwing suspicion onto Morris, and then blackmailing him. Fay, of course, didn't realise what her friend was up to.

JEFFREYS: It's my bet she thought someone else was going to be the victim.

YATES: I agree, Jeff. Anyway, the plan was put into operation. Fay bought a scarf exactly like the one worn by Morris. She made it perfectly clear when she was buying it that it was a present for a very wealthy friend of hers. The telegram – which was sent by Mr A of course – confirmed the impression that Clifton Morris was the wealthy friend. Later, Morris's scarf was stolen and – I imagine – destroyed.

MATTHEWS: So the scarf which Fay bought was the one …

YATES: (*Interrupting him; nodding*) With which she was strangled – yes. It was imperative, of course, that the scarf should eventually be brought to our notice and identified as the one which Fay had presumably given to Morris.

MATTHEWS: And it was Miss Hastings who identified it?

YATES: Yes; but I think she was in two minds about it. It was only after four or five days' deliberation that she decided to do what Mr A wanted.

MATTHEWS: Which was to identify both the scarf and Terry Morris?

YATES: Yes. Unfortunately for Miss Hastings, you saw her in Regent Street, and her story about Chamonix was blown sky high.

MATTHEWS nods. There is a tiny pause.

MATTHEWS: Inspector …

YATES: Yes?

MATTHEWS: Would you say then that Miss Hastings had taken the place of Fay Collins?

YATES: No. I think Miss Hastings had been working for Mr A for some considerable time. I think she'll go on working for him.

JEFFREYS: Why do you think that, sir?

YATES: Because she's scared to death of him, Jeff – and he intends to keep it that way.

MATTHEWS: (*To JEFFREYS*) I think he's right, Sergeant. Remember the shooting incident, only the other day …

YATES: Yes, and the Diana Winston murder; it's my bet that really put the fear of the devil in Miss Hastings. (*Suddenly; offering MATTHEWS his hand*) Well, thank you once again, Padre. You've been a very great help.

MATTHEWS rises and shakes hands with YATES.

177

CUT TO: *MATTHEWS comes out of the Police Station and gets into his car which is parked by the kerb. He is just about to drive away when JOHN HOPEDEAN appears, walking on the pavement, past the car. He is carrying the large canvas folder. He looks at the car and recognises MATTHEWS.*

HOPEDEAN: Hello, Padre!

MATTHEWS: Good morning, Mr Hopedean. Would you like a lift?

HOPEDEAN: Are you going to Littleshaw?

MATTHEWS: Yes.

HOPEDEAN: Then I certainly would!

MATTHEWS: Jump in!

MATTHEWS leans across and opens the passenger door. HOPEDEAN crosses in front of the car and gets into the passenger seat next to MATTHEWS.

CUT TO: YATES' Office at Littleshaw Police Station. Day.

YATES is sitting at his desk, writing a letter. The door opens and JEFFREYS enters.

JEFFREYS: Excuse me, Mr Collins is here; he'd like a word with you.

YATES: (*Looking up*) All right, Jeff, bring him in.

JEFFREYS nods and goes out. YATES finishes his letter and puts it in an envelope. JEFFREYS returns with EDWARD COLLINS.

EDWARD: Good morning, Inspector.

YATES: (*Pleasantly; indicating a chair*) Hello, Mr Collins. Sit down, sir.

EDWARD: No, I won't keep you a moment, I just happened to be passing …

YATES: (*To JEFFREYS*) Don't go, Jeff.

178

EDWARD: I got your message about being able to
               show my face in public again, and I
               thought …

YATES: (*Laughing*) Oh, yes! Thank you very
               much, sir – I'm very grateful. It was kind
               of you to help me.

EDWARD: Yes, but I'm not quite sure how I did help
               you, Inspector.

YATES: Aren't you, sir?

EDWARD: No. You simply asked me to stay indoors
               for three or four days and not see anyone.

YATES: That's right, sir. (*Smiling*) You remember
               the fight you had with Mr Morris?

EDWARD: It wasn't exactly a fight, Inspector.

YATES: No, sir – but you were knocked
               unconscious.

EDWARD: Well?

YATES: Well, I let Mr Morris think you were dead
               – that he had, in fact, murdered you.

EDWARD: (*Amazed, staring at YATES*) Are you
               serious?

YATES: Quite serious.

EDWARD: Well, what good did that do?

YATES: It scared the pants off him and made him
               talk. You see, for one horrible moment, he
               thought he was a murderer. (*Looking at
               EDWARD; quite simply*) And strange
               though it may seem, Mr Morris isn't a
               murderer, Mr Collins.

*EDWARD looks at YATES, then at JEFFREYS, then back
at YATES again.*

EDWARD: Well, if Morris didn't murder my sister –
               who did?

179

YATES: (*After a moment; rising and coming round the desk to EDWARD*) Ask me that question at the end of the week, sir. I shall probably be able to answer it by then.

EDWARD: (*A shade surprised; and puzzled*) Yes, all right, Inspector.

EDWARD shakes hands with YATES. The telephone rings, and JEFFREYS lifts the receiver.

JEFFREYS: (*On the phone*) Hello? … no, this is Sergeant Jeffreys … Hold on, please.

YATES is showing EDWARD out of the office.

YATES: How's your leg these days, sir?

EDWARD: It seems better just recently. If I can borrow a car I shall probably start driving again.

YATES: Oh, good. (*Quietly; almost confidential in manner*) Ring me at the end of the week, sir.

EDWARD looks at YATES, still obviously puzzled, then turns and goes out of the office. YATES closes the door and looks across at JEFFREYS, who is still holding the telephone.

JEFFREYS: (*With his hand over the mouthpiece*) It's Clifton Morris. I think he's heard something …

YATES quickly crosses towards the telephone.

CUT TO: Hammersmith Bridge. Day.

CLIFTON MORRIS is standing on the bridge, looking down the river. He turns and sees an approaching police car. MORRIS is obviously expecting the car. He moves to the edge of the pavement as the car slows down. The rear

180

door of the car is thrown open, and MORRIS quickly jumps in. The car drives away.

CUT TO: Inside of the Police Car. Day.

MORRIS and YATES are sitting side by side.

YATES: (*Briskly*) Well – what happened?

MORRIS: A woman telephoned me …

YATES: When?

MORRIS: Last night – about eleven o'clock. She said she was a friend of Kim Stevens'.

YATES: Go on …

MORRIS: She said she'd get me the letter if I'd pay eight thousand pounds for it.

YATES: What did you say?

MORRIS: I said I would.

YATES: (*Nodding*) Good. Go on, Mr Morris …

MORRIS: She's calling at the flat tomorrow afternoon.

YATES: What time?

MORRIS: She said some time after three.

YATES: How do they want this money – in notes?

MORRIS: Yes.

YATES: Get the money from the bank tomorrow morning.

MORRIS nods.

YATES: You know what to do. Play it perfectly straight. Take the letter and simply hand over the bank notes.

MORRIS: (*Nodding*) Yes, all right. What happens when I've handed over the money?

YATES: (*With a little smile*) You fade out of the picture and leave the rest to us. (*Still looking at MORRIS*) That's an order, sir – you understand?

181

MORRIS: Yes, I understand, but I'm not very good at
             taking orders, Inspector.
YATES: (*Quietly; still looking at MORRIS*) This is
             one you've got to take, sir.
MORRIS: (*After a moment; with the suggestion of a
             smile*) Inspector, if someone has been
             blackmailing you – if someone had made
             you look like a murderer – would you
             want to fade out of the picture, without
             knowing who that person was?
YATES: You'll know, sooner or later, sir.
MORRIS: You still haven't answered my question?
YATES: (*Smiling*) You can't go by what I'd do, sir;
             I'm a pretty unorthodox sort of character.
             You must have realised that by now.

*MORRIS looks at YATES, then points his finger at him,
and his thumb at himself.*

MORRIS: You, and me too, Inspector!

CUT TO: The Front Door of CLIFTON MORRIS' Flat
in the carpeted corridor. Day.

*A gloved hand appears and presses the doorbell. The
camera tracks back to show MARIAN HASTINGS facing
the front door, a large cream hatbox in her hand. The
words: MARIAN HASTINGS, Littleshaw, are prominently
displayed on the hatbox. After a moment the door is
opened by CLIFTON MORRIS.*

MARIAN: I think you're expecting me. I telephoned
             you on Tuesday night.

*MORRIS looks at MARIAN for a moment; she stares back
at him.*

MORRIS: You'd better come in.

MARIAN enters the hall.

CUT TO: The Drawing Room of CLIFTON MORRIS' Flat. Day.

MARIAN enters, carrying the hatbox; she looks round the room. MORRIS follows her.

MORRIS: Now look, before we go any further, I want to make perfectly sure that you've got the letter.

MARIAN: You know I've got it. Kim Stevens showed you a photostat.

MORRIS: That doesn't prove anything.

MARIAN: Well, it must prove something, Mr Morris. You can't take a photostat of a letter you haven't got. However, perhaps you'll find this more convincing.

MARIAN opens the hatbox and takes out a spool from a tape recorder, and also an envelope.

MARIAN: This is the tape you heard: that's the envelope your letter was in.

MORRIS picks up the envelope and looks at it.

MARIAN: Well, are you satisfied?

MORRIS: This is the envelope, yes – but where's the letter?

MARIAN looks at him, then slowly taps her handbag. MORRIS hesitates, then turns and goes into the bedroom. After a moment, he returns with an attaché case which he puts down on the table, and then opens it. MARIAN looks inside the attaché case. There are bundles of pound notes neatly stacked side by side inside it. MARIAN opens her handbag and takes out a letter which she hands to MORRIS. MORRIS moves away from the table and opens the letter. MARIAN starts to transfer the notes from the attaché case into the hat box. MORRIS thoughtfully reads the letter. After a moment, he slowly puts it into the envelope, and puts the envelope in his inside pocket.

183

MARIAN closes the attaché case, having transferred the notes from the case into the hatbox. She looks at MORRIS, then picks up the hat box, and turns towards the hall.

MORRIS: (*Quietly*) Wait a moment …

MARIAN: (*Turning*) Well?

MORRIS: (*Indicating the hat box; ironically*) What do you get out of this? (*Moving towards MARIAN*) He's blackmailing you, isn't he? We're both in the same boat, aren't we, Miss Hastings?

MARIAN: (*Tensely*) What are you talking about?

MORRIS: What's your price. A letter? A photograph? A forged cheque, perhaps?

MARIAN: (*Angrily; tense*) That's my business!

MARIAN turns and goes out into the hall. MORRIS stands looking towards the hall until he hears the closing of the front door, then he moves across to the table, picks up the telephone, and dials a number. After a moment, we hear the number ringing out on the other end of the line.

JOCK: (*On the other end*) Hello? … Falstaff Garage …

MORRIS: (*On the phone*) Jock – this is Mr Morris. I want the Bentley.

JOCK: Okay, Mr Morris …

MORRIS: Straight away, Jock – I'm in a hurry …

JOCK: It's on the way now, sir …

CUT TO: A side street in Littleshaw. Day.

This street runs at right angles to the main street – the High Street of Littleshaw. Various shops, in the main street, can be seen, including MARIAN HASTINGS' establishment.

CLIFTON MORRIS' Bentley is parked in this street and MORRIS is sitting in the car, watching the dress shop. He looks at his watch, and then glances up again; as he does so MARIAN's car arrives on the scene and draws to a standstill in a vacant space in front of her shop. A GPO Telephone (Service-Repair) Man arrives in the main street at the same time as MARIAN's car; it parks on the opposite side of the road, facing MARIAN's shop. MARIAN gets out of her car, carrying the hatbox, and goes into her dress shop.

CUT TO: MARIAN HASTINGS' Dress Shop in Littleshaw. Day.

EDWARD COLLINS is stood talking to PHYLLIS, who is working on a dress at the centre table. MARIAN enters, carrying the hatbox.

PHYLLIS: ...There used to be a little woman over at Amersham, but whether ... Oh, here's Miss Hastings. Perhaps she'll be able to help you.

MARIAN: Why, hello Edward! This is a surprise!

EDWARD: (*Turning*) Oh, hello, Marian ...

PHYLLIS: (*To MARIAN*) Mr Collins has got several of his sister's dresses he wants to get rid of, Miss Hastings. He was wondering if we could help him?

MARIAN: (*To EDWARD*) Are they here, Edward, or at the flat?

EDWARD: Oh, they're here – I've had everything brought down from Town.

MARIAN: Oh, I see.

EDWARD: There seems to be an awful lot of stuff; three or four coats, five or six evening gowns ... I just don't know what to do with them.

185

MARIAN: Well, of course, I can't take them, Edward, but there's a little woman over at Amersham who might help you. She won't pay you much, though, I'm afraid …

EDWARD: I'm not worried about that. I just want to get rid of the stuff.

MARIAN: (*Crossing towards her office*) I'll give you her phone number and you can give her a ring.

EDWARD: Oh, thank you.

MARIAN goes into her office with the hatbox. PHYLLIS continues working on the dress. EDWARD stands watching her. After a moment, MARIAN returns without the hatbox, but with a piece of notepaper in her hand.

MARIAN: (*Offering EDWARD the notepaper*) Here we are Edward. This is the address and the phone number. I think you should drop her a line, if I were you – she's not frightfully good on the phone.

EDWARD takes the note, reads it, then looks at MARIAN.

EDWARD: Yes, all right, Marian. Thank you very much. (*To PHYLLIS*) Goodbye …

PHYLLIS: Goodbye, Mr Collins.

EDWARD looks at MARIAN again, puts the note in his pocket and goes out of the shop.

MARIAN: (*To PHYLLIS; a shade tense*) Has Mr Goodman telephoned?

PHYLLIS: (*Shaking her head; still working on the dress*) No, there's no messages. It's been very quiet …

CUT TO: ALISTAIR GOODMAN arrives in his shooting brake. The brake is parked near the GPO van and GOODMAN gets out of it and crosses the road.

186

GOODMAN stands for a moment, looking in the tobacconist's next to MARIAN'S establishment.

CUT TO: *Two policemen are in the GPO van – PC MARTIN (in uniform) and DETECTIVE SERGEANT HARRISON. MARTIN is sitting at a shortwave (police) radio transmitter. He holds a hand microphone and wears earphones. HARRISON is watching the dress shop and the main street through a small side window in the van.*

HARRISON: (*Turning*) Tell them Goodman's arrived on the scene. He's looking in the tobacconists.

MARTIN nods and presses the switch down on the radio receiver.

CUT TO: A police car parked in a side lane at Littleshaw.

YATES and JEFFREYS are in the front of the car: two uniformed men in the back. JEFFREYS is holding a hand microphone.

JEFFREYS: (*To YATES*) Goodman's turned up.

YATES: (*Nodding*) They know what to do …

JEFFREYS nods and raises the microphone to his mouth.

CUT TO: *We see GOODMAN through HARRISON's eyes for a moment and then the camera tracks in as GOODMAN turns away from the shop, very casually looks up and down the High Street, and then goes into MARIAN's shop.*

CUT TO: MARIAN HASTINGS' Dress Shop. Day.

PHYLLIS is still working on the dress when GOODMAN enters the shop. MARIAN is in her office.

GOODMAN: (*To PHYLLIS*) Hello, Phyllis!

187

PHYLLIS: (*Turning*) Oh, good afternoon, Mr
               Goodman.
GOODMAN: Is my Lord and Master in?
PHYLLIS: (*Smiling*) Yes, I'll fetch her. (*She gets off
               her chair*)
GOODMAN: Have you been to the flicks this week?
PHYLLIS: No.
GOODMAN: Oh, you've missed a beauty! Just your cup
               of tea. All about a little boy who runs a
               white slave gang and smokes marijuana.
PHYLLIS: I thought it was a prison film?
GOODMAN: It is. His old man slaps him and gets two
               years.

*PHYLLIS gives GOODMAN a look. MARIAN comes out of
the office with a hatbox in her hand.*

MARIAN: (*Handing her fiancé the hatbox*) Here we
               are, Alistair …
GOODMAN: Oh, jolly good!
MARIAN: You know the address?
GOODMAN: Yes, rather …
MARIAN: It's awfully kind of you, Alistair – I do
               appreciate it.
GOODMAN: (*Kissing MARIAN on the cheek*)
               Nonsense! (*Turning towards the door*)
               Don't be silly, old girl. (*He winks at
               PHYLLIS*) But don't expect me to make a
               habit of it.

*GOODMAN grins at the pair of them and then goes out of
the shop.*

CUT TO: *MORRIS's eye-view of MARIAN's dress shop
sitting in the Bentley. He sees GOODMAN comes out of
the shop, carrying the hatbox. He crosses to the shooting
brake, puts the hatbox on the passenger seat, and then gets*

into the car. MORRIS leans forward in his car and turns on the ignition key; his eyes still on GOODMAN's brake.

CUT TO: *ALISTAIR GOODMAN's brake leaving the High Street at Littleshaw, followed by MORRIS's Bentley.*

CUT TO: A country road near Littleshaw. Day.
There is a field on the extreme right, with an open gate and a cart track leading down to a barn.

GOODMAN's car passes the entrance to the field and continues down the road. MORRIS's Bentley is following GOODMAN's shooting brake.

CUT TO: *GOODMAN's brake draws to a standstill outside the main gate of a large country house. GOODMAN jumps out and crosses to the back of the car. He opens the two rear doors and is taking a brace of pheasants out of the car when MORRIS's Bentley drives past. GOODMAN looks up, casually noticing that MORRIS is looking at him. MORRIS's car continues down the road.*

CUT TO: *MORRIS has driven the Bentley off the road and is parking it down a side lane. He gets out of the car and cautiously walks towards the main road in the direction of GOODMAN's brake.*

CUT TO: *GOODMAN's brake is still parked outside the large house. MORRIS is approaching the brake. As he does so we see a large noticeboard near the drive of the house. The wording on the board reads: Littleshaw Orphanage. Patron: Lord Bronrich. Hertfordshire County Council. MORRIS stares up at the noticeboard. Curious,*

189

and a little puzzled, MORRIS turns and walks round to the front of the shooting brake. Suddenly, and to his obvious surprise, he notices that the hatbox is sitting on the front seat of the car. He looks across at the entrance to the orphanage and quickly opens the car door, takes out the hatbox, and removes the lid. Inside the hatbox is a woman's hat. MORRIS looks up and finds that GOODMAN has appeared and is stood watching him.

GOODMAN: What the devil do you think you're doing?

MORRIS: I'm sorry – I didn't think there was a hat in there, I thought …

GOODMAN: (*Taking the hatbox from MORRIS*) I don't care what the hell you thought! What right have you … (*He stares at MORRIS*) I've seen you before somewhere, haven't I?

MORRIS: (*Tensely; with authority*) Look, tell me – has Miss Hastings got an appointment this afternoon?

GOODMAN: (*Puzzled*) Yes, I think so …

MORRIS: (*Taking hold of GOODMAN's arm*) Where?

GOODMAN: I don't know where – in Littleshaw, I think …

MORRIS releases GOODMAN's arm and starts to run down the road in the direction of his car. GOODMAN stares in amazement, then slowly replaces the lid on the hatbox.

CUT TO: *MARIAN climbs out of her car carrying the hatbox. The car is parked off the road, on the grass verge, near the entrance to the field and the barn. She goes through the gate and down the cart track towards the barn. Suddenly a small car can be seen parked on the extreme left of the track and partly hidden by the hedge.*

190

We recognise the car – it belongs to MATTHEWS.
MARIAN takes no notice of the car, although she has
obviously seen it, and continues down the track towards
the barn.

CUT TO: Inside of the barn. Day.
This is an isolated barn which is used chiefly for storage.
There are several bales of straw; an old handcart; two or
three empty barrels; and a considerable number of sacks
containing both potatoes and artificial fertiliser. The
entrance to the barn is down on the extreme right, past a
dilapidated manger. Several implements: a billhook, spade,
hoe, etc, are on the floor near the manger.

MARIAN comes into the barn carrying the hatbox. She
looks tense and worried and moves slowly down towards
the bales of straw. She stands for a moment looking round
her; puzzled by the fact that the barn appears to be empty.
As she puts the hatbox down on a bale of straw, a sound
suddenly attracts her attention, and she swings round and
looks towards the entrance. There is a pause. The figure of
a man gradually appears at the opposite end of the barn
and moves slowly towards MARIAN. As he approaches, we
recognise JOHN HOPEDEAN. He wears a dark lounge
suit, with a scarf draped round his shoulders.
HOPEDEAN: You're late.
MARIAN: (*Tensely*) Did you borrow that car outside?
HOPEDEAN: Yes; from Matthews. For obvious reasons
                   I didn't want to use my own. (*Smiling*) He
                   thinks I'm spending the afternoon at the
                   Tate. (*Moving towards the hatbox*) I began
                   to think you weren't coming, Marian.
MARIAN: I had difficulty getting away.
HOPEDEAN: Were you followed?

MARIAN: No. No, I don't think so.

HOPEDEAN: You don't think so? (*Looking at MARIAN*)
            Aren't you sure? It's always nice to be
            sure, you know, on occasions like this.

MARIAN: (*Tensely; a shade angry*) I've told you – I
            don't think so!

*HOPEDEAN looks at MARIAN; then looks inside the
hatbox.*

MARIAN: It's all there – you needn't count it.

HOPEDEAN: I've no intention of counting it; not at the
            moment, at any rate. Did you have any
            trouble with Morris?

MARIAN: No, I simply gave him the letter – he
            handed over the money.

HOPEDEAN: (*Smiling*) I see. Nice and simple. It's very
            much pleasanter when it's nice and simple,
            isn't it, Marian? Unfortunately, it doesn't
            always work out that way.

MARIAN: (*Suddenly, tense, facing HOPEDEAN*)
            Why did you murder Diana Winston?

HOPEDEAN: I should have thought that was obvious.
            She was going to provide Morris with an
            alibi. To say the least, that would have
            been a disastrous state of affairs.

MARIAN: I told you I wouldn't stand for another
            murder!

HOPEDEAN: I know. I know what you told me, Marian.
            I hadn't forgotten.

MARIAN: (*Tensely*) Then why did you do it?

HOPEDEAN: I've told you why.

There is a pause.

MARIAN: (*Frightened, but determined*) John, I've
            made up my mind. I'm going to the police.

HOPEDEAN looks at MARIAN, obviously surprised.

192

HOPEDEAN: (*Softly*) What do you mean? What are you talking about?

MARIAN: I'm going to tell them exactly what happened that night. I'm going to tell them that I knocked someone down with a car and that I – I didn't stop.

HOPEDEAN: And that you were drunk, Marian. Don't forget that. Don't forget to tell them that you were drunk.

MARIAN: (*Quietly; shaking her head*) I shan't.

HOPEDEAN: But my dear Marian, it's over a year since that woman died. What good do you think it's going to do if you go to the police now?

MARIAN: It will stop you blackmailing me.

HOPEDEAN: Oh, I'm sorry you feel that way about it. I thought our association was a very happy one. (*Taking hold of MARIAN's arm*) Why, we've had some very nice times together, Marian – very nice.

MARIAN: (*Releasing her arm; softly*) I'm going to the police.

HOPEDEAN: Then at least you must satisfy my curiosity. What are you going to tell them when they ask you why you waited twelve months before giving yourself up?

MARIAN: I shall tell them that I was frightened.

HOPEDEAN: And that you were being blackmailed?

MARIAN: (*Quickly*) No! No, of course not! I shan't mention that … I daren't mentioned it because if I did …

HOPEDEAN: (*Interrupting MARIAN*) Our nice Mr Yates would start putting two and two together. (*Slowly pulling the scarf down from his*

193

shoulders) And something tells me he's
very adept at putting two and two together,
Marian.

*MARIAN looks at HOPEDEAN, then suddenly makes a
dash towards the door: but HOPEDEAN is anticipating
the move and springs between the bales of straw and the
manger. MARIAN backs away from him; nervous and
frightened.*

HOPEDEAN:(*Holding the scarf*) You silly little fool …
How stupid can you get? … Do you think
I'd let you go to the police? (*Moving
towards MARIAN*) Do you think I'd let you
set foot in Littleshaw after this?

*MARIAN makes a wild dash for the opening between the
sacks and the bales of straw, but HOPEDEAN catches her
and swings her round towards him. MARIAN attempts to
scream but he puts his hand over her mouth and quickly
slips the scarf round her throat.*

CUT TO: *The Bentley is racing down the road towards
Littleshaw. Suddenly MORRIS sees MARIAN's car on the
grass verge. He brakes; the Bentley comes to a standstill,
and MORRIS jumps out of the car and crosses the road.
He stares at MARIAN's car for a moment, and then moves
down towards the field.*

CUT TO: Inside the Barn.

*MARIAN is still struggling with HOPEDEAN; suddenly
she digs her fingernails into his hand and for a brief
moment he releases his grip. As he does so MARIAN
makes a last desperate effort to pull the scarf from her
throat. She is struggling with HOPEDEAN and the scarf
when MORRIS runs into the barn. HOPEDEAN turns,*

recognises him, and quickly grabbing one of the implements from the floor, jumps towards MORRIS. The two men struggle for a brief moment, then disappear behind the bales of straw. Suddenly we see the implement being raised in HOPEDEAN's hand, followed by a blow, then a groan from MORRIS. MORRIS falls to the floor, semi-conscious; HOPEDEAN breathlessly stares down at him. Suddenly HOPEDEAN turns and looks at MARIAN. She is leaning against the wall of the barn; terrified and exhausted. The scarf is on the floor. HOPEDEAN makes a quick decision; grabs the hatbox and runs towards the far end of the barn and the exit.

CUT TO: *HOPEDEAN comes out of the barn, carrying the hatbox, and runs towards the small car – MATTHEWS' car – parked near the hedge. Before he reaches the car, however, two police cars race through the gate and brake to a standstill inside the field. HOPEDEAN quickly realises that in order to escape he must now abandon any thought of using the small car and makes direct for the road. He can see MARIAN's car and the Bentley through the hedge. He races past the two police cars as men pour out of them into the field: just as HOPEDEAN reaches the entrance a third police car appears from off the road and completely blocks the exit out of the field. YATES, JEFFREYS and two uniformed men jump out of the car and advance towards HOPEDEAN. HOPEDEAN turns and then realises that the group of men from the other police car are advancing on him. He drops the hatbox and dashes back in the direction of the barn. This move has been anticipated, however, by the first arrivals, and the circle merely widens with HOPEDEAN still in the centre of it. HOPEDEAN stands tense; frightened; watching for an opening in the circle. Gradually, the ring tightens with the police advancing towards him. Finally, in desperation, HOPEDEAN makes a dash for the gate again, but the police close in on him.*

CUT TO: Outside the Barn.

MARIAN is leaning against the door of the barn; hand on her throat. JEFFREYS joins her.

JEFFREYS: Miss Hastings, I must ask you to come down to the station with us.

MARIAN nods and, swaying slightly, moves away from the barn. JEFFREYS takes hold of her arm. YATES races past them and goes into the barn.

CUT TO: Inside the Barn.

MORRIS is slowly rising to his feet as YATES enters. YATES takes hold of MORRIS's arm and helps him across to the bales of straw. MORRIS leans against the bales, slowly regaining his breath. He still looks dazed.

YATES: (*Concerned*) Are you going to be all right, sir?

MORRIS: Yes ... Yes, I think so ...

YATES: I'll tell Jeffreys to get a doctor ...

MORRIS: No ... No, I'll feel better in a moment. (*He looks at YATES*) Did you pick him up?

YATES: Yes.

JEFFREYS enters.

JEFFREYS: (*To YATES*) Everything's under control, sir. The cars are just leaving.

YATES: (*Nodding*) Right!

JEFFREYS: (*To MORRIS*) Are you all right, Mr Morris?

MORRIS doesn't answer; but gives a little nod.

YATES: He'll be okay …

JEFFREYS: Harry, when did you first suspect Hopedean?

YATES: Some little time ago. He was just a little too frank for my liking; just a little too sure of himself. So when he told me about those poison pen letters I decided to send him one.

JEFFREYS: (*Surprised*) <u>You</u> did?

YATES: Yes. But I didn't call him a murderer. Oh, no! Nothing so crude. I called him a filthy blackmailer and accused him of blackmailing Miss Hastings and Mr Morris.

JEFFREYS: But he didn't tell us about that letter …

YATES: No; he made a mistake – he should have done. But it was too near the truth for him to risk it.

MORRIS looks at YATES and gives a little smile.

YATES: Well - are you feeling any better, sir?

MORRIS: Yes, I'm all right now.

YATES: (*Smiling*) Well, don't expect any sympathy, Mr Morris. I warned you, didn't I? I told you to fade out of the picture.

MORRIS: (*Rubbing the back of his head*) I was beginning to think I had …

YATES laughs.

CUT TO: The country road near Littleshaw.

Three police cars, followed by MARIAN's car – driven by a uniformed policeman – emerge onto the road.

197

HOPEDEAN is in the first car; MARIAN is in the second. The cars drive down the road and out of the picture.

CUT TO: Outside the Barn.

MORRIS and YATES are walking away from the barn. In the background, JEFFREYS can be seen coming out of the barn, carrying HOPEDEAN's scarf. He hurries towards YATES and MORRIS.

JEFFREYS: (*To MORRIS: holding the scarf*) Excuse me, sir – is this yours?

MORRIS looks at JEFFREYS, then at YATES.

MORRIS: (*Smiling*) I don't expect either of you to believe me, but the answer's – no!

YATES: (*Taking the scarf from JEFFREYS; laughing*) We believe you, sir!

JEFFREYS nods to YATES and MORRIS and crosses to the small car parked near the hedge. YATES and MORRIS continue walking towards the road.

CUT TO: A country road near Littleshaw.

MORRIS and YATES are walking across the road towards the Bentley; YATES still holding the scarf.

THE END

The Press Pack

... press cuttings about The Scarf

The BBC Television Film unit which has been using Windsor for some of its location shots during the last few days for a new Francis Durbridge series has run into several difficulties.

Several shots were taken on different days. Producer Alan Bromly explained that some would have to be re-filmed and were supposed to have been taken by the river. But flooding made this almost impossible.

The series is planned to run in six half-hour episodes. The first part of the serial, "*The Scarf*" will be screened on February 9th.

Local viewers should be able to recognise Windsor High Street, a part of the Guildhall, as well as Jane Grey's gown shop. Action of the play takes places in "a sleepy market town some 30 miles from London."

But it will be called "Littleshaw" instead of Windsor and Jane Grey's will becomes "Marian's". The dress shop is an important part of the plot.

Alan Bromly is the son of former Slough Borough Engineer, Mr Alan Bromley, sen., who retired from his post in 1939, lives at 14 Upton Park, Slough.

Leading parts in the series are taken by Stephen Murray, Lockwood West, Patrick Troughton, Donald Pleasence and Diana King.

Windsor Express

On February 9th, Stephen Murray appears in the first episode of a new Francis Durbridge thriller which will keep him on the BBC TV screen for six weeks.

The mystery, by the creator of Paul Temple, is called "*The Scarf*". It is Murray's third appearance in a Durbridge tv serial. The others were "*My Friend Charles*" and "*A Time of Day.*"

This is one production about which I can reveal nothing. To do so I would have to break open the six-inch thick safe in which the scripts are kept until a week before each episode. They will be handed to the cast one part at a time.

Says producer Alan Bromly, "I believe the cast are better off if they are kept in suspense like the viewers. A villain will appear much more innocent if he doesn't know he's the villain until the last instalment and that's no reflection on anyone's acting ability."

The Evening Telegraph and Post

If you've any flesh left to creep after Quatermass and his ape-men, ghosts and demons have stopped monkeying about – then thriller writer Francis Durbridge hopes to raise some goose pimples.

His new whodunnit serial, called "*The Scarf*" is to start on BBC TV on February 9th. I wish you joy putting the jigsaw pieces together.

Nobody knows better than Durbridge how to complicate a story and hide clues so effortlessly. Producer Alan Bromly is one of a handful of people who knows the solution and he swears we're in for a tough time finding the villain.

Something of a team are Bromly and Durbridge. They've worked together on four such serials already – *"Portrait of Alison,"* *"My Friend Charles,"* *"The Other Man,"* and *"A Time of Day."*

As soon as the script is finished Bromly grabs it. The final episode is placed in a secret hiding place and the cast are kept guessing like everyone else.

So it's no good asking Stephen Murray, playing a wealthy publisher, Oscar winner Donald Pleasence, playing a detective, Vilma Anne Leslie, cast as a cabaret star, or Leo Britt for a private tip-off about the ending.

Blonde, 24-years-old Vilma Anne Leslie secured the glamour role because she "read" the part so well at an audition.

Liverpool Echo

I've always thought of Francis Durbridge as one of the finest manufacturers of red herrings in the whodunnit business.

His subtlety is drawing attention away from the man who really slipped the cyanide into the rent collector's beer has been tantalising, infuriating and entertaining audiences for nearly a quarter of a century now.

The subject of red herrings came up during the weeks when Britain's master of the mysterious and I were discussing his latest serial, *"The Scarf"*, which begins on BBC TV on Feb 9th.

"I never sit down and try deliberately to bring red herrings in," he said surprisingly. "I write from the point of view of the people in the story. According to the sort of people they are, they behave in certain ways, some suspicious, some not. It's the viewer's interpretation of

201

this behaviour that creates the red herrings, not me at all."

Durbridge admits that to write the kind of stories which have brought him acclaim and considerable fees, you not only need a special technique, but a certain kind of mind. He says: "I never base my plots on real-life mysteries. I see excitement in small things that other people might call trivial and I build on them. Something in my mind clicks as soon as I see a small thing which points to something unusual."

Francis Durbridge, who resembles a successful businessman rather than one of his own heroes as some people see him, began writing for television eight years ago.

"Partly," he explains, "because I was interested in the medium, and partly to identify myself as myself and not Paul Temple."

For *"The Scarf"*, a straight murder mystery which takes place in Littleshaw, a market town 30 miles from London, and in the soft lights and smoky atmosphere of London's clubland, producer Alan Bromly has collected a formidable cast. Donald Pleasence, Stephen Murray, Patrick Troughton among others.

I'm willing to bet my Sunday boots that a shoal of red herrings will be swimming around as well.

News of The World

Once more the guessing game is on at the BBC Television Centre. It is all about the latest "whodunnit".

Naming the culprit is the problem which faces actors, technicians, secretaries – even the tea boy – concerned

202

with the production of Francis Durbridge's new thriller serial, "*The Scarf*", which starts tomorrow night.

Only two men know the answer, Durbridge himself and producer Alan Bromly.

"*The Scarf*" opens with the finding of the body of a girl in a market town a few miles from London.

The action moves between the tranquil surroundings of the town and the rarified atmosphere of a West End Night Club.

"A lot of people in the production until now may think they may know who is the murderer," said Mr Bromly when we met yesterday.

"But no matter how hard they may try to worm out the secret Francis and I refuse to give it away."

Mr Bromly and Mr Durbridge are old associates in the art of leading viewers from their sitting rooms and up the garden path.

Between them, they have found the formula which can keep an audience of many millions well on its toes and guessing almost to the last line or two.

Now I am one of those many characters who thoroughly enjoy being in the know. I find it much more fascinating to watch a thriller when I know the killer's identity. I like to look on while the author works out the problem.

I explained all this to Mr Durbridge and Mr Bromly. They were immensely unimpressed. Smilingly, Mr Bromly replies, "If that's the case then you are going to hate "*The Scarf*"."

Mr Durbridge nodded approval before adding, "Try as you will we are just not talking."

So I tried actors Stephen Murray and Donald Pleasence.

They are the stars of the story. Mr Murray plays a wealthy publisher. He shook his head. Could a man who loves books kill a pretty girl?

Perhaps not. And Mr Pleasence, winner of the best television actor award for last year, is the police inspector, so surely it couldn't be the friendly looking Mr Pleasence.

An artist is also involved, and we all know what a Bohemian lot painters can be. He is played by Leo Britt, just back in Britain after acting for ten years in America.

But Mr Britt did not know if he had been cast in the murder role.

I gave up the hunt convinced only of one thing, the murderer is certainly not lovely Miss Norrie Carr, Tynemouth model and actress. She plays the girl who is strangled, so at least that lets her out.

Sunday Sun, Newcastle-on-Tyne

Francis Durbridge has so many radio and television successes behind him that a new serial from his able pen is bound to be a television event. His latest, "*The Scarf*," began last night, again with Stephen Murray in a leading role and again produced by Alan Bromly, and it shows all the signs of being another cunningly contrived "whodunnit."

It was not long before the body was produced. The victim was a beautiful actress found, of all unlikely places, lying on top of a load of hay when a startled farm labourer rolled back a tarpaulin. It is a bit early yet to start spotting the villain, for the finger of suspicion is swivelling

204

in all directions like a compass needle vainly seeking north. It points at Stephen Murray, whose shoes seem to be a clue; at Patrick Troughton, who radiated mystery; at young Anthony Valentine, who finds the scarf that presumably did the deed in his violin case; at Bryan Coleman, the farmer; and even at Diana King, who seemed just a little too plausible.

Yes, Mr Durbridge is busy again leading us along the garden path – though this time perhaps it is the farm track.

Eastern Daily Press

Unless you are a "Wagon Train" fan, BBC-TV holds most of the trumps on Monday night, though the re-entry of "The Larkins" does strengthen ITV's hand.

However, not even Peggy Mount and David Kossoff could keep me away from the new Francis Durbridge serial on BBC-TV, and I was not disappointed. Has Mr Durbridge ever written a thriller serial that was a flop? If he has I can't recall it, and "*The Scarf*" promises to be another winner.

It was off to a cracking start, jerking us into the story right away. Without the slightest fuss we were introduced to as nice a selection of Durbridge characters as you could wish to meet including, of course, a body.

Such a craftsman deserves a good cast, and Mr Durbridge gets one here, with top-line television actors in Stephen Murray and Donald Pleasence in the lead and such players as Patrick Troughton and Lockwood West in support.

This is at least one safe half-hour for five more Mondays ahead.

Telegraph and Argus, Bradford

Francis Durbridge, the BBC's Agatha Christie, has me under his spell again. His eighth "whodunnit" for TV started last night.

This means that for 30 minutes on the next five Mondays, I – and countless other viewers – will sit near-tortured on the edge of my seat trying to solve the riddle: "Who Killed Fay Collins?"

Actually Det-Insp Yates, a new name in the ranks of TV 'tecs, is in charge of the case, but he'll get bags of assistance from us amateurs all over the country, as do the numerous other screen sleuths.

"*The Scarf*" as this serial is called, kicked off in typical Durbridge style. A farm hand pulling back the canvas on top of a hay load and hey presto! there was the beautiful Miss Collins as dead as a doornail. Strangled by The Scarf.

Immediately clues and leads poured into Yates' office: we met all the characters concerned and by the end of Episode One we were all completely baffled.

Heaven knows how we'll fare after five episodes. Most of us will probably have forgotten what we are trying to solve, but it will have made our Monday evenings.

Mr Durbridge recently completed 21 years of Paul Temple spine-tinglers for sound radio. I think that listening to a Temple series is better than watching Mark Saber, Martin Kane, Mike Maguire and most of TV's smart-Alecs.

Why wouldn't Temple have been put in charge of the Collins case? Incidentally, "*The Scarf*" takes the place of "*Quatermass*" as our Monday evening blood-chiller. Give me Mr Durbridge every time.   **Bristol Evening World**

As *"The Scarf"* completed its first loop last night it was tightening into a noose around the neck of suspect No. 1.

But, as Francis Durbridge devotees knows well, it is sure to slip a few times before the knotty problem is unravelled.

With plays like *"Little Red Monkey"* and *"Quatermass"* the six-part serial has become a Lime Grove speciality, and no one has done more to make it "blue plate" than Durbridge.

His approach – creepy, everyday incidents which suddenly assume sinister proportions – make it easy to believe "it could happen to me."

Added to which Durbridge wastes no time with a build-up. He pushes forward the plot with clues which cancel each other out with bewildering speed.

Donald Pleasence, 1958 television Actor of the Year, is the chief unraveller of *"The Scarf."* He is unlike any detective-inspector I ever met, but his poker-face style smoothes over mere physical incongruity.

Newcastle Journal

BBC television's new thriller in six parts, *"The Scarf"* opened as promisingly last night as one would expect on finding Francis Durbridge the author. He is now in his 22nd year as the sound radio detective Paul Temple, his own creation.

"The Scarf," his eighth crime serial for television, is a pure "whodunnit" opening, very properly, with the discovery of a girl's body in a quiet market town near London. It is a cosy, gentlemanly piece with actors who seem interesting in themselves.

Their alert, wary demeanour may have to do with a report that Alan Bromly, the producer, has forbidden the cast to look at the script of the final episode. No one knows who will turn out to be the villain.

So far the odds are against Stephen Murray, as a Mayfair fashion magazine publisher on whom suspicion rests at present. It may be that he acts all the better for not knowing himself.

This production is a first television serial for Donald Pleasence, well cast as Det.-Insp. Yates. There is something about his quite scholarly manner suggesting that Sherlock Holmes would have approved of him.

Daily Telegraph

Francis Durbridge's policemen stick in your mind, but Detective-Inspector Yates who is wrestling with "The Scarf" mystery is the best so far. Unmistakably he is one of us, a man who has not always been successful and is taking no chances this time; and when he suddenly shows that he has not one but many things up his sleeve, is in fact in masterly control of the situation, we feel hugely gratified – we are doing splendidly.

How much of this subtly provided satisfaction is due to Mr Durbridge, and how much to Donald Pleasence's wonderful, wry, dry playing, I'm not sure. There were times in earlier episodes when Mr Pleasence threw away so many of his lines that there was hardly a man left in the middle at all; and other moments when the wisdom of casting Stephen Murray as the effective victim in two such serials running seemed doubtful, the concentration on him as the scarlet herring to the exclusion of the mere red ones almost unprofessional. But now all these doubts are gloriously resolved and the betting heavy on the vicar or the artist as the real villain. Or could it be the farmer?

Glasgow Herald

Have you made up your mind who killed Fay Collins? Author, producer and cast of "*The Scarf*" the final episode of which you will see tonight, have received scores of letters from viewers giving what they think is the solution of the riddle. But Alan Bromly, the producer, tells me that in the letters he has seen nobody is quite definite. "They name one person," he said, "then add, if it's not him it is so-and-so."

As is customary with a Durbridge serial, the cast do not know who the culprit is until they are given their final scripts after transmission of Episode 5. But, says Mr Bromly, they do pick up ideas through appearing in it week by week.

"One thing that sometimes gives them a clue, though often a misleading one, that filming of exteriors of all six episodes is done before the opening of the serial. It is often difficult to do this without giving away "who done it." For instance, an actor may have to do a scene where he is chased and caught which immediately gives him the idea he is the culprit. Of course, he may be wrong.

"One reason why we do not tell anybody who is the murderer is because innumerable people throughout the country run sweepstakes on the result."

For the first time in a serial of this kind the cast have not run their own sweepstake on the result.

"I think it is because it is a much larger cast and they have not all appeared in every episode," he said.

209

Audiences for "*The Scarf*" has been about the same as for "*Quatermass*," averaging approximately nine million.

Incidentally, the intriguing little film that introduces the serial – the scarf that appears to float and then straighten itself in front of the viewer – is done with the aid of a wind machine and a high-speed camera.

The scarf is held taut in front of the camera while the speed of the wind machine is increased until it catches the scarf and blows it away. The film is then reversed and run through at quarter-speed.

Nottingham Evening News

Well, who did it? You will know tonight if you have the makings of a detective. Like everybody else you must have been watching Francis Durbridge's thriller serial "*The Scarf*" which now comes to the end of a highly exciting six weeks.

Who is your suspect – Clifton Morris, Marian Hastings, the Rev. Nigel Matthews, Alistair Goodman or John Hopedean?

Durbridge and producer Alan Bromly have resolutely refused to divulge the identity of the culprit – and not even the player concerned knew until they started to rehearse this week's episode.

But tonight justice is done.

Press & Journal, Aberdeen

Printed in Great Britain
by Amazon